A SPLASH OF RUBIES

A SPLASH OF RUBIES

Virginia Coffman

This first world edition published in Great Britain 1998 by
SEVERN HOUSE PUBLISHERS LTD of
9–15 High Street, Sutton, Surrey SM1 1DF.
This first world edition published in the U.S.A. 1999 by
SEVERN HOUSE PUBLISHERS INC of
595 Madison Avenue, New York, N.Y. 10022.

British Library Cataloguing in Publication Data

Coffman, Virginia, 1914-
     A splash of rubies
     1. Romantic suspense novels
     I. Title
     813.5'4 [F]

     ISBN 0-7278-2240-3

Typeset by Hewer Text Ltd
Edinburgh, Scotland.
Printed and bound in Great Britain by
MPG Books Ltd, Bodmin, Cornwall.

One

T hroughout the night gypsy wagons rattled up the cobblestones of the little Yorkshire street toward the moors beyond the village. Their noise aroused many of the villagers, who peered out between the warped shutters of the dark little houses to catch a glimpse of the colourful procession.

Some of the observers, including the local physician, Dr Halperin, had marked the date of the seasonal gypsy horse fair for different reasons: there would be more work for him, and it was sure to bring out the village's only local gypsy, whose Irish beauty and strange, gypsy excitement had secretly attracted him since his arrival in the village almost five years ago.

Shortly after dawn he arose, washed, dressed and went to the street door of his small office, eating a chunk of gingerbread 'moogin' in lieu of breakfast. He watched the procession for some time but failed to see what he hoped to find. The woman hadn't come out of her little house yet.

One of the gypsies, bringing up a late wagon, called to him. "Ah, friend, we've come by once more. Do we see you at our horse fair?"

1

The doctor waved back. "Greetings, friend. You may see me if you aren't too busy cutting each other up."

This was a standing jest, because the tribe was usually set upon by locals who found they had been sold something less than an animal of the first breed. But the gypsy only grinned, flashing his white teeth.

Several gypsies waved their big, dark hats to the doctor as they passed by with their families of silent, dark-eyed women, and inquisitive, eager children who said nothing either, but looked at everything. Nevertheless, the gestures of the males were an indication that they accepted him, something they neither had done nor would do for the rest of the doctor's fellow citizens.

The last of them shouted, "There'll be the best in horseflesh, shawls and trinkets. Jewels and fairings for your females."

Halperin knew the only gypsy who lived in the area was responsible for their trust in him. The beautiful Irish gypsy, Samara Connel, would pass his office shortly on her way to join the fair, and if he was lucky, with no patients at hand, he might exchange a few words with her.

He was sure other males in the village shared his secret fascination with her but, like Dr Halperin himself, they could never forget her mother's people.

However, there was no harm in exchanging a few words with her now and again, or even satisfying himself with watching her, wondering what it would be like to make love to a heathen gypsy. It was just as

2

well not to wonder, at his age. He would never see forty again, and Samara Connel could scarcely be twenty-two.

One of the more sober sheepmen came out of the Black Dog Tavern which theoretically closed at midnight, but permitted some of its better customers to sleep off their night of ale and rum fustian. The sheepman called, "You'll be making no profits from me today, Doctor. My woman is demanding I take her to the gypsy fair."

Dr Halperin smiled. "Got to keep a steady head and hand if you're going to out-cheat those lads."

The sheepman raised both hands, palms out in surrender. "The problem's not with the horse-traders. It's with my daughter and her mother, buying every *fairing* that's offered or given. And the fortunes that Samara Connel will promise them. Nigh on Christmas she sold my daughter a love potion to use 'gainst Jamie Bostich, him that drinks his way home the nights when he an't off in the tavern's back parlour snoring."

The doctor watched him go on down the street. He resented the fellow's way of speaking about Samara Connel, but was perfectly aware that he himself felt much the same way about the green-eyed Samara's potions and the nonsense she sold the gullible when her gypsy friends passed this way once or twice a year.

But some time had passed and the gypsy hadn't come by, though the camp was already set up. Other matters must come before conversations with the gypsy girl. He had better see to the care of his office. Once the fair opened, there would be the beginnings of quarrels about spavined horses and conterfeit money, and ultimately knife fights. That meant business for Dr Halperin, often bloody business.

He looked up the street toward the gaudy brightness of the fair and the newly decorated gypsy wagons. No sight of her among the busy workers of the fair. But suddenly, his hopes raised as he turned toward the lower end of the village where the street made a sharp left and plunged downward toward the valley below. At the turn of the street Samara Connel had come out of her little one-room house and started up the cobblestones which were too steep and slippery for the horses of the area, but were routine exercise for the villagers.

She could be seen at almost any distance in her Sunday gown, though she didn't attend the local church. The dress was full-skirted, totally unlike the dainty, light outfits most of the young females with money had worn since Waterloo and peace had come. And he had no doubt that anyone as sharp as Samara had money hidden away, aside from the coins she wore like a heathen on her person.

Even at this distance the satiny green of her skirt was sure to bring out the deep black of her eyes, and on most women would have clashed with her gold blouse and deep pink sash. The low neck that revealed a noticeably rounded bosom seemed a shocking custom to the doctor, but fortunately it was somewhat covered by the faded shawl she wore with ease and grace. She was not yet wearing around her thick, dark hair the bandeau of gold pieces but would fasten it on later in the day. The bandeau, she had told him once, was her entire fortune. Normally worn sewed to her petticoats, the coins were her estate from her mother's people. He thought it dangerous and told her so but she had only laughed.

He wondered if she carried a dagger with her. He wouldn't put it beyond her.

Samara Connel's walk always fascinated him. There was nothing male about her except the lengthy stride that had a surprising swiftness. The air was sunny but chill and blew her hair freely about her high-boned cheeks.

Dr Halperin had been half-concealed, standing in the doorway, but she saw him. Knowing how the gossip spread about her if he went out to meet her, he let her come across the cobbles to him.

"Coward!" she chided him. "You are afraid you will be cheated. Aren't you going to visit the fair and show them how clever you are at bargaining?"

Wryly frank with her he said, "I am a poor man, Miss Samara."

He was one of the few villagers who called her 'Miss' but his careful politeness did not seem to impress her. She shrugged and her shawl slipped down from her shoulder. He caught a glimpse of the olive-gold flesh but that didn't trouble her either. She raised the old, faded shawl on her shoulder and reminded him in a manner that teased but warned, "Come to the tinker's wagon and buy a charm for your love. I'll give you a fairing for her, old friend."

She was laughing when she left him and did not see

him wince, but she was sure to sense that her remark had reminded him of his age.

She was beautiful, he agreed. But she possessed a gypsy's devilish nature, and no matter what his desires might be, he knew they would receive no genuine response from her.

What would happen to her among those strange people who shared only half her blood?

Going back into his small office, he wished he could know what the fascinating creature's end would be. Nothing pleasant, he guessed. Perhaps he would wander up to the horse fair this afternoon and learn what he could about her behaviour among her own kind. No doubt, at this moment, she was laughing over her treatment of him, imagining in some strange way that she had made herself his equal by her independence.

Poor creature!

Two

With the experience of many years the gypsy band had camped on the only level field, just where the cobbled street ended and the rolling moors began. It was far from the most interesting section of the moorland. Samara usually passed it with little interest during her long, enjoyable walks over the moor to the next village where she sold fortunes, trinkets and potions.

She was not inclined to socialise with the pale-fleshed people who had always regarded her as 'different', 'heathen' and 'thieving'. Early experience as an alien child in her Christian grandmother's coteen had taught her to be content amid the hidden creatures of the moorland world. Time and spidery patience had shown her that she was a solitary creature herself, like the denizens of the moorland and an occasional sheep-herder's family who also called the moors their home.

She was friendly but indifferent to those around her. She welcomed the gypsy band from which her mother had come but when their wagons had rattled onward, she was not lonely. The moorland was always there.

The Prince Regent, carrying on his lively affairs in

London and Brighton, had no notion that the king and queen of this little alien band regarded themselves as quite foreign and superior to his subjects. According to their beliefs, their lives, rules, punishments and religion were in no way subordinate to the British throne.

Having lived here so long, Samara found this amusing and even innocent. She could almost, if not quite, see both worlds at the same time.

She found the old tinker's wagon waiting for her as usual. Both Stefan and his wife, Marika, the band's leaders, were related to her mother in some intricate way dating back back hundreds of years. On her mother's death they had paid her Irish grandmother for the wagon and on occasions like the present visit to the North of England it was understood that Samara should have the use of the still useful tinker's wagon, with its cutlery and sharpening stone, its kettles, pans, grilling rock, besides the blankets and other items occasionally replaced by the good-hearted Marika.

The band was usually too busy setting up the fair to do more than greet her at this point in the day, but that did not fool her. They cared. The Romany looked after their own and considered themselves far older in the human race than Christians and other 'newcomers' to the universe.

Today, however, Samara was surprised to find Marika climbing up the steps of her wagon and peering into the dark interior, her heavy, once pretty face looking anxious. Samara came up behind her and called, "What, friend? Has one of your ewe lambs concealed itself behind my crystal ball?"

Startled, the woman looked behind her, saw Samara, and backed down the wooden steps, complaining in the Romany tongue, her hips swaying in their full pink satin skirts.

"Worse. My boy, that dog of Satan, has made off with some young female. Barely seventeen he is, and the girl fifteen. And he talks of true love."

Samara understood Marika's concern if the matter reached anyone from the nearby towns who would certainly like nothing better than a chance to drive the band out of the area, at the least or, more dreaded by the band, imprisoned far from the freedom of a wanderer.

"I'll find your boy, Marika," she promised, confident as usual. "You go and help Stefan with the dancers costumes."

Marika looked around reluctantly. "You will be gentle, Samara? He is so young."

Young, Samara thought. *I'd lay about his young hide with my bare hand. You have been too easy with Alexi.* But she didn't say it aloud.

"Yes, Marika. I'll be gentle. Go now."

There were other Christian girls, some barely in their teens, who had been fascinated by the dark, alarming eyes of the Romany. But from birth Stefan's band were taught the deadly danger provided by that youthful and often naïve temptation.

Samara left the tools of her profession in the wagon, locked it and strode around the stamped-down grass of the enclave. She walked past the silk and satin streamers over various wagons, hardly aware of the exotic noise of guitars and braying animals which had already collected the admiring chatter of village youth.

She had a knowing and cynical eye for the young girls who sneaked up from the village to whisper and giggle. They pointed out the various young men whose piercing black eyes seemed to stab through them but oddly enough made no overtures toward them.

Was I ever that young? Samara wondered.

Probably not.

Seventeen years ago, on the evening she arrived in the Yorkshire village of Heaton Clough, in her grandmother's care, she had held herself tightly to reveal nothing of the child who had lost both her mother and father, and that free, exciting world across the Irish Sea.

In Ireland she had been used to genuine fatherly attention from the Romany males. Nothing else would have been permitted. She still remembered the tightrope artist who had believed himself irresistible. His efforts to kiss her throat and childish breasts when she undressed in the wagon had aroused her to a rough, shocked battle royal, involving some furious bites.

She had excellent white teeth.

She never knew what happened to the tight-rope walker after Marika heard the struggle and rescued her, but she was relieved not to see him again, and was proud when she could fight off any drunken lout during her youth with her grandmother in Heaton Clough.

Her grandmother had been more disgusted than shocked when the twelve-year-old Samara confided to her of battles with local youths.

"A decent child would not entice these poor lads in the village. I might have known how it would be when my own boy actually married one of your – one of those heathens."

After that, Samara took care never to confide in her or anyone else of her race. As for passion, nothing she had experienced thus far in life was worth the sly, knowing glances of the females in the village, who watched her as though she might reduce their ignorant, wayward boys to the level of gibbering idiots.

She occasionally wondered what kept her here when the Continent must be free now to those Christians, Romanies and all the rest, since the Peace. She had only to earn a few more guineas, more gold pieces. She didn't require much of a wardrobe, and there would always be the gypsy camps. She could earn her way in the gypsy fashion.

The Romany had to help each other against a hostile world. Besides, Marika and Stefan had friends everywhere. She must only take care to avoid the places where they were feared or hated, for there were certainly dangers in the cities and countryside from which this band had emigrated to the Isles.

She had thought to find Alexi and his doubtless pretty Christian pullet around the instrumentalists who were practising behind one of the tents. A little further away the rope walkers and tumblers practised last minute tricks before the awed crowd, but most of the first group from the village consisted of men looking to bargain with the experienced gypsies over a trained mare, a pony, or a team in good condition to carry women over the moors to Leeds and York.

The juvenile sound of giggling, punctuated by a teasing young male voice gave Samara a clue to the whereabouts of Alexi, but as she turned a corner she came instead upon the husky, grizzled Stefan, vehemently arguing the qualities of a mare in reasonably good shape, an opinion with which Dicken Parks, the owner of the Black Dog, did not agree.

The boyish sound she had heard was obviously one of the Romany youths listening to the debate. The chances were that the men would soon come to an agreement. At this hour bargains could be made for both parties before the best stock had been picked over.

Musicians were strumming, to the delight of the village youths and their sweethearts, but there was no sign of Alexi and the girl. Samara decided the idiotic boy had daringly coaxed her into one of the wagons.

Moving in her swift way, she swung around, and her heavy skirts, dappled with coins of low currency, lashed against the trim figure of a stranger in a beaver hat and a greatcoat. A gentleman, from the look of him.

He reached out and steadied her, then, seeing that she was unhurt he let her go abruptly and rubbed his lower thigh through the folds of his greatcoat. While she framed a polite but brief apology, he looked her over. Indicating her skirts, he said, "You have a useful weapon there. Do you always carry your estate with you?"

She took a breath, finding his remark condescending
and impudent. He would never have dared to say that
to one of his own kind.

"Only when I do not expect to meet with—"

"Clumsiness?"

His mouth, sensuous and not unattractive, curved as
if he would smile, but it was hard to read his hazel eyes.
They were less than friendly. She suspected he had the
usual prejudices of his kind against hers and stepped
back in order to go around him.

Whether he was amused or not she refused to be
embarrassed. After all, he was on Romany territory
for the moment.

He put out a hand to detain her.

"I won't keep you. I know how you people feel
about us. But I seem to have mislaid a young lady. My
ward."

Suddenly uneasy, she softened her manner and
suggested, "Perhaps she is eating bon-bons. Young
people usually head there first."

"That was what she said she would do," he confessed. "But I'm afraid the child's word isn't worth a
farthing. I was discussing a business matter with an
acquaintance in the village yonder and when I reached
your horse fair she was nowhere in sight."

She could say only, and with reason, "I am very
sorry. But my people won't hurt her. She is safe here."

"Your people?" He gave her a wry and doubtful
look. "But she spoke to a young – person in Leeds. It
was at some distance from me, but he may have been a
gypsy, and quite possibly they made some sort of

assignation for this place. I should have had my attention on her instead of the damned business."

She hurried to end this suspicion, though it was very likely true.

"Let me search for the young lady, sir, at the west end of the grounds. You might try the east where the young people stand about eating those little Turkish rolls."

She did not like the way he was studying her. Despite his physical attractions, unusual in a visitor to the horse fair, she would have liked to send him as far away as possible. There was a minute when she feared he would ignore her suggestion and she added, "Our fair has always appeared here. The magistrate of this district gave us permission. He will tell you of our rights if you are not familiar with them."

This time he did smile. It was not a smile she would easily forget. Unexpectedly warm.

"That won't be necessary. As it happens, I am Sir Anthony Linden. I am by way of being a magistrate myself."

Shocked, she forced an answering smile.

"Well, sir, I wish you good fortune. If I find your ward I will bring her to the tent beyond the entrance stakes."

He looked over at the flaring pennons at either side of the entrance.

"Thank you. I shall expect her there, if I do not find her myself. Meanwhile, very likely, I shall come upon her."

Obviously he did not trust her to bring the girl to him. However, he removed his hat and stood there watching her until she left him. Was this a sudden and unexpected sign of respect? She could only hope so. His dark hair was a trifle unruly in the wind and made him look less arrogant. Or perhaps it had been his smile after all. But that was gone now. He looked thoughtful, which did not reassure her.

She noticed that he took the opposite direction from the one she had pointed out. Meanwhile, the guitarist and a dancer who had stopped their rehearsal while she talked to the stranger now returned to their work, but they too had been worried by the conversation.

All strangers might be potential enemies. Worse. The man was a magistrate, a Justice of the Peace, and these authorities were all important. They could order the band to prison or transportation for almost any fancied crime.

Samara tried not to dwell on that too much. She could only wish profoundly that the missing little ward would be found at any minute – and not in a compromising position with Alexi.

Having searched the camp, all she could do now was spread the word among the wagons and busy workers, all of whom knew the importance of locating the truants. They didn't have to be told the danger of a magistrate's presence in their midst.

By the time she reached her own wagon, somewhat to her surprise, the area before the door was almost deserted, unlike most occasions when there would be several women or young girls waiting to have their fortunes told.

Marika was waiting for her. "I sent them away. I

was afraid you might bring my boy and that troublesome little witch to the wagon."

"No. By the by, a magistrate is here. He is the
guardian of Alexi's love."

Marika rolled her dark eyes. "I'll have the girl back
or break Alexi between my bare hands."

Worried as she was, Samara laughed while Marika
scrambled down from the wagon steps and trotted
across the grounds.

Samara went into her wagon, got out her veil and
the chaplet whose coins glowed from much polishing
as they would be worn in her dusky hair. She put her
crystal ball on the little table before her with its
cabalistic signs. These were her theatrical props and
although faint shafts of lamp light glowed myster-
iously in the heart of the ball from beneath a hole
in the centre of the table, she used her own wits and
imagination to promise her customers what they
wished for – when she didn't send them away shivering
at her dire warnings of danger.

She then made a stately progress the length of the
wagon interior to summon back the first of her clients.

To her astonishment there was only one person
waiting for her to open the door, a pretty, childish
girl of fifteen or so, with hair like pale flax and
enormous blue eyes. She looked up at Samara, smiling
like a mischievous child.

"Two women came but I sent them away. May I see
you now, miss?"

Samara had dealt with mischievous children before
and recognised tricksters no matter what their age

16

might be. Very possibly, this was the missing ward who had been captivated by the roguish Alexi.

She would be more than glad to find out the truth. In the long-practised, deep voice that had served her well, Samara said, "They are searching for you. You must go to them. Evil is upon this camp."

The girl put a fine, gloved hand to her mouth. "You know?"

"I know."

"But I must have my fortune told. We are to go back to London; my guardian's business is finished in the North. And when we are home I will never see my beloved again."

It would seem that Alexi had a great deal to answer for. Samara remained firm. "You must go home."

The girl wailed, "You don't understand. I'll never see him again. My guardian will have me shut away in some awful place."

Samara wanted to say, "Rubbish!" but the girl was obviously working herself into a state and wavered, reaching out for Samara's support.

"I was running from Alexi. Just a joke. And I lost him, so I thought I could have my palm read or whatever you do. And maybe you'd show me the way back to him. But I'm so tired. If I could just sit down a few minutes. Then I will go. I promise you."

The girl squeezed past her up to the top of the wagon's steps and seemed about to push her way into the interior of the wagon, but she swayed again and Samara caught her, leading her to the cot that served as a bed inside the wagon.

"Sit down. Breathe deeply."

"It's very dark," the girl whispered. "Frightening." She seated herself gingerly on the cot. Then she fumbled in her reticule, murmuring, "If I could have some water . . ."

She looked around, clearly finding the place unnerving, and spied some bon-bons and jellies that Marika had left for Samara. "I'll have a couple of these and some water. Then I may be able to face Cousin Anthony. He's my guardian. If I am very good, he may not notice too much what I feel for my wonderful Alexi." She reached into the pewter dish and took another of the bon-bons. Again she murmured, "I'm so thirsty."

"There is no water," Samara told her firmly. "Shall I pour you some wine? It is better for you."

The young lady agreed that this would be satisfactory. Pouring the wine, Samara wondered how much of the girl's childishness was real and how much was acting. She put the pewter cup into the girl's hands, which began to tremble but recovered as she drank.

She looked up, her eyes full of gratitude. "Must I really go now? What if he is very cross? He frightens me sometimes. He was in the wars, you know. In Belgium, and he's just returned from Waterloo."

"I'm sure he wouldn't choose to be your guardian if he didn't care for you."

The girl looked up innocently. "Oh, but sometimes he is ever so nice. Then, other times, it's quite frightening."

"Nonsense. Come along."

Beginning to absorb some of her new friend's confidence, the girl's spirits were raised. "Maybe Alexi and I will run away instead of staying at Cousin Anthony's house? Alexi can be very persuasive."

I don't doubt that, Samara agreed, but silently.

"Oh, yes. He wants to take me away across the Channel."

"What!"

There would be the devil to pay, involving the entire band, if the boy carried off a magistrate's ward. They would hardly get as far as the Channel, but while nothing would happen to the romantic-minded girl, the camp would find itself accused of stealing a child, the penalty for this being death on the gibbet.

In view of all this romantic dreaming, Samara said coolly, "I suggest we return to your guardian first, miss. You will find it rather expensive to travel about the Continent without a small fortune."

"Yes, I know," the girl murmured sadly.

Samara pushed open the wagon door and finished as they went out on the steps, "A deal more funds than your gypsy sweetheart would be able to lay his hands on, no matter how skilled he may be."

The girl had hurriedly swallowed her second bonbon and tightened her clasp on Samara's arm just as Samara saw Sir Anthony Linden standing at the foot of the steps looking up at them.

Obviously, he had heard her and no longer doubted that Samara was contributing to his ward's dangerous dreams. The contempt with which he addressed her was all too clear.

19

"How obliging! You have found my ward. Come along, Dilys. No more gypsy adventures for you today." He held out his hand. To Samara's surprise the girl broke from her arm and let Sir Anthony help her down the steps.

"Oh, Cousin Anthony, thank you! I was so frightened. I kept walking around in circles."

"Well, your adventure is over now." He looked up at Samara. "Good day. Better luck elsewhere."

Samara longed to answer him in kind, but did not dare. She was grateful that the matter had ended without serious trouble.

She watched Sir Anthony and Miss Linden start out, the girl clutching his arm and looking up pitifully to complain, "I don't feel well, cousin. I don't feel well at all . . ."

Wondering how much of the girl's feelings were genuine, Samara went back into the wagon, took up the gold and green robe, then the veil and chaplet, and made ready to greet the more superstitious village females.

Three

S amara's fortune-telling held ironic barbs that day. She was relieved that Sir Anthony had not yet pressed some charge against the band. There was always a chance that he would do so another day, but it did not seem as likely now that he had recovered Dilys.

Nevertheless, when one eager nail-biting young seamstress from Keighley asked Samara if her wish would come true, Samara refused to see an easy answer in her crystal.

"It is not wise to dwell on that particular wish without more proof. Let a second wish be hinted at."

This confused the seamstress, which was Samara's intention, but the young woman's companion, a bonnet-trimmer, translated.

"I see what it is. You must linger over the expensive bonnet but choose the new hat. It will be all the rage and less dear as well. That should impress him."

Highly satisfied, the girls left the wagon giggling.

Questions asking whether one was loved were usually all too common but the area of Heaton Clough was much more interested in money, sheep, whether a sale would pass, and whether the next child would be a male or female.

It was the latter which Samara thought of as her Greek Oracle question. She answered enigmatically.

"I see within the light a contradiction. It will not be what you believe in your mind, but that which will make you happy all your years."

Having spent several hours at this task, which took more imagination than skill, she closed and locked the wagon and went off to rekindle her romantic answers and sharpen the others.

The fair, under windy blue skies, was at its height and she had to wait in a laughing, gossiping line before Marika's open tent where the sauce-filled Turkish rolls were selling briskly.

Beside Samara, Marika's big husband, Stefan, stood with his crinkling hair whipping in the breeze. He ate two rolls while he thanked Samara for managing to locate the missing Dilys Linden.

She shook her head. "Actually, she came to me." She added, "But you must keep your boy away from Sir Anthony's ward. The lad has ambitions in that direction."

Stefan spat out some Levantine seeds from the roll, just missing Samara's skirts. Grinning, he made a sweeping gesture of denial.

"Not our lad. I know Alexi has a new female every night. But he would never dare touch a magistrate's ward. He is not that kind of fool."

He *was* that kind of fool, Samara thought, as he had demonstrated several times, but she looked over at

Marika who was busy rolling up more Turkish delicacies. Stefan, seeing this, said as he always did, "Marika will take a whip to him. She knows Alexi."
Samara doubted if whips would tame the sexually active boy who was even now eating a roll to which a girl of the band treated him. He saw he had aroused Samara's attention and his fine, delicate lips widened in a satisfied smirk.

Samara turned her attention elsewhere, wondering at the same time if Alexi really would dare to steal off to Europe with a prominent English magistrate's ward. It was not like him to make such a bold move. He was far from heroic.

She said firmly to Stefan, "The stupid girl has hinted at running away with your son. If you are willing to hang, I am not."

Stefan's heavy features shifted into a scowl.

"No. You are right. We will send him back to Dorset before the wagons leave York. He has a couple of young females there. The love of his life, he swears."

"Both of them?"

He shrugged. "One is rich. My lad likes that in a female. And he has lusty appetites as well."

Samara realised she would have to speak to Marika after all, though she did not know how much good it would do. Unless Marika completely lost her temper, the boy would tease her out of punishing him.

Meanwhile, Samara hoped that she herself had seen the last of the young potential troublemakers. She knew that Marika and Stefan and the band regarded the wild heath of Dorset as their home, and if Alexi persuaded Sir Anthony's ward to go there with him he and the band would be in even more danger than if he made off with the girl to Europe.

Young Alexi, having finished his Cornish pasties and Turkish rolls, removed the gypsy girl's hand from his arm. He followed Samara on her way across the grounds to the area fenced off from the rest of the wagons, tents and the livestock area. The centre of the fenced square was where Samara read the Tarot cards for those who paid sixpence. The band had learned long ago just how careful the wives of the local sheepmen were with their hard-earned money and Samara considered sixpence generally what the Tarot fortune was worth.

Alexi sauntered around the fence to the entrance where one of Samara's young apprentices collected the fees while listening with some excitement to the promise of past and future by the ancient and exotic cards. Alexi reached casually for the girl's hair, in which were braided cheap, sparkling beads. She pulled away in annoyance and without the insinuating smile Alexi was used to. Obviously, she took her work very seriously.

Annoyed, Alexi tried to push by her to enter the little Tarot square. Samara had seated herself on a high-backed oaken chair before a Queen Anne-style gaming table that someone had 'acquired' before Samara was born. Already teenage girls were gathering to pay their fee, followed by their elders, who pretended a laughing disbelief in the whole process.

Samara looked up at Alexi, her eyes expressionless.

A Splash of Rubies

"I see nothing in the cards for you. When you have sixpence come back and fall into line." On several occasions in the last year or two he had tried to make trouble at the beginning of her readings. She had ignored him before, but it was time she ended this childish humour.

Alexi's dark skin tightened. "I can pay. And buy whatever else you sell." He reached in the slit pocket of his embroidered vest and tossed down several coins, all of them silver.

Samara suspected he had obtained them from Sir Anthony's ward or stolen them and was now foolishly exhibiting them before gossiping witnesses.

She said quickly, "I know you won them from gambling so take them and be off."

The nearest girls giggled, and then gasped as Alexi brushed the coins off the table, attracting more attention to his little horde. At least, Samara thought, the idea of gaming winings was perfectly acceptable at a horse fair.

The coins showered Alexi's sandals and he muttered something in Romany that made the girls look puzzled and nervous, probably expecting either Alexi or the Tarot fortune-teller to pull out a dagger.

Samara had no difficulty in understanding the youth, but she knew him well. He swallowed hard, and seeing another boy vault over the fence after the coins, he brought his sandal down hard on the groping hand of the intruder. The intruder was one of the band and had the good sense to retire and let one of the girls commiserate with him.

When Alexi arose and glanced at Samara, his lips broke into a forced grin. "Well, then. Who wants your Tarot reading, hag!" and he backed away toward the fence. Samara was amused to see him stop long enough to wink at one of the girls before he left the square. This scene meant harder work in order to register the proper mood for the hopeful and eager females, not to mention a sprinkling of youths who jeered at each other's belief in such doings but did not leave the line that formed.

Though Samara managed to see a deal more good than bad in the cards, half of her mind was occupied with the fear that Alexi had actually stolen the coins from Miss Linden. But a more obvious answer occurred to her. Dilys had boasted to Samara that the boy wanted to run away with her to the Continent. It was unlikely that anyone with those hopes or plans would steal from the girl. Upon a pretence of needing money for some plan of their own, he had doubtless persuaded her to turn over some of her money to him.

Samara felt better with this solution, although she knew it did not mark the end of the relationship between Alexi and Dilys. She concentrated upon the cards, which turned up with more cheerful promise for the eager and excited group, three-quarters of them female, who kept her busy during the afternoon.

As the wind stirred up clouds and whistled over the moorland distances, Samara was relieved when the fair began to empty of those who came from villages further away and wanted to cross the moors before the weather worsened.

A Splash of Rubies

She began to put away all the paraphernalia that represented a gypsy band to these villagers and was surprised to see the thin, greying village doctor walking toward her.

Usually Dr Halperin was reticent about being seen gossiping with her, but now he moved in haste, paying no attention to the villagers who watched him curiously and put their heads together. No doubt finding fresh matter to gossip about.

He said formally, "Miss Connel, you are wanted in the village. I thought it best if I came for you. It's about a Miss Linden. I believe you were with her this morning?"

She looked up, inwardly shaken but determined as ever not to show this to the physician, even if he was the band's special *'gadjo'*.

She asked with her cool smile, "Was that her name? The child came to me for her fortune but her father – no, her guardian, I believe – came to fetch her."

"Yes. Sir Anthony is her guardian. A gentleman of some importance at court. Acquainted with the Prince Regent."

Dr Halperin tried either to oblige her or hurry her by picking up one of her cards that had fallen. It was The Hanged Man, a card she always tried to avoid. She shrugged and slipped the card in with the other tools of her trade.

"Well, come along then."

Four

Walking beside Dr Halperin, and often a step ahead of him, Samara firmly refrained from asking questions until she found a way to indicate that she herself felt no guilt whatever.

As they started down the cobbled street she asked with mild curiosity. "How may I help this child?"

He was all business. The shy fellow hiding in doorways was gone and he meant to play his role as Heaton Clough's single authority upon the matter at hand.

"Sir Anthony is a cousin of some kind, home from the wars. He was at Waterloo. He comes home to find himself guardian to the young lady you met. He tells me her mother died while he was in Belgium and he finds himself in sole charge of his cousin's child."

"His care of her is not ideal. Young ladies of her class are always accompanied by an abigail. A maid."

"Ah, yes. They lost her in York. It seems she objected to our climate. They intend to borrow an abigail from their next host, General Roxburgh,"

"I don't envy the unfortunate woman."

He hesitated, then blurted out, "You see, he thought you might have noticed the young lady's ear-bobs.

Heirloom rubies. One of them seems to have been lost by the young lady. The tiny ribbon that secured the jewel slipped off. They don't believe it was stolen, but someone may have found it, where she lost it. At the fair, of course."

This sort of thing was not foreign to Samara. As soon as a jewel of any kind was lost, they thought of the 'gypsy fortune-teller' of course.

"I know nothing of her ear-bobs. I didn't notice that she was wearing any."

He frowned. "No accusation has been made, you understand. Nothing of that sort. But the jewel may easily have come off when she was drinking the wine in that tinker's wagon of yours."

"Then let her go back and trace her steps. How would I know where she lost it?"

"Because, by coincidence, she remembers touching it when she was waiting to see you. But she has had a bit of stomach trouble since she left the fair. I advised her to sit quietly in my office until you and Sir Anthony return with the jewel. By that time, she should be quite herself again. Personally, I think it was your wine that affected her. A child like that probably is used to ratafia or some other mild drink."

She smiled. "Of course. The Wicked Gypsy makes her drunk on wine and when the poor young miss is confused and loses her precious jewel, the Wicked Gypsy takes it. Isn't that my popular role?"

He became anxious at her misunderstanding. "No, no, no, Miss Samara. Nothing of that sort. It was only that you are more likely to find it, perhaps when you are removing your things from the wagon, and you might not know to whom it belonged."

"We know now, though, don't we?"

He was so relieved that he did not read beneath her sarcasm and laughed at what he regarded as a joke. "It is part of an heirloom set of rubies that will go to Sir Anthony's bride when he marries. He permits the child to wear them."

The wind whipped around Samara, lashing her bright green and gold skirts against her body. She pulled her faded green shawl over her wildly blowing hair and held the ends under her chin with her free hand. Cold as it was, she wanted to keep on walking until she reached the tiny wool-spinner's house that had belonged to her grandmother. She wanted no further contact with the Lindens.

They came to the doctor's office, likewise once used by spinners, who would sit in the bow window that gave a clear view of the street and the gutter where most of the villagers generally walked. Samara braced herself for the inquisition ahead, wondering if by chance the troublesome Alexi had anything to do with Miss Linden's vanished earring. If he did, it would make her own position even more difficult.

The doctor's office and living quarters were small and crowded with the various tools of his trade. A shaving bowl held some unpleasant but clean instruments that might be used by a barber. There was a covered basin on the floor near the casement window on the side of the room and Dilys was dabbing her lips with one of the doctor's reasonably clean towels before she replaced the cover of the floor recepticle. Evidently, she had either choked or spat out something. Samara felt secure about the candies Marika had left for her, and she herself had drunk the wine and had no bad results. But if the girl was really sick, had Marika and the others been serving food that was old or otherwise impure?

Sir Anthony helped his pale and trembling ward to a chair under the window. When Dr Halperin hurried to Miss Linden her guardian said calmly, "It seems to be nothing but nerves. However, if you can give her something to calm her stomach—"

"Cousin, don't say stomach! Besides, I must have left the ear-bob in – or around – the gypsy wagon, because that's the last time I felt it."

"When she was eating, of course," Sir Anthony explained to Samara. "She is a greedy little puss." To Samara's relief he did not sound like her accuser. "Thank you for coming in this weather."

Upon being acknowledged by him, Samara would have curtsied briefly but he held out his hand, as though to shake her own. She extended her ungloved fingers which he took in his.

"Strong fingers, beautifully shaped," he said, to her astonishment, and that of the doctor. Sir Anthony's wartime service had made him surprisingly free with his compliments to strange females. She was unexpectedly pleased and her fingers felt heated in his palm, as she herself was warmed by his smile. She lost her easy indifference and pride for the moment.

"The wind has come up, sir," she said in answer to

his remark. "We Yorkshire folk weather it out." She gave him a low, teasing laugh. "We are very proud of our strength."

"She was so kind to me, cousin," Dilys put in, bringing them back to the matter at hand. "Those lovely bon-bons and such good wine. Not that I am familiar with wines, but it must have been a splendid vintage. Isn't that what they call it?"

"If the young lady is not used to wine," Dr Halperin suggested, "even a small amount may be oversetting."

Samara was puzzled and uneasy again. "I don't understand. Has Miss Linden lost a piece of jewellery because of something she ate at the fair?"

Dr Halperin was examining the lace-trimmed handkerchief Miss Linden had given him, and Sir Anthony looked over at the doctor.

"Nothing there? Dilys, tell me, what else did you eat at the fair besides Miss Connel's wine and bon-bons?"

"Well, there were the Turkish rolls. We both—"

Samara held her breath at this mention that seemed a plain reference to Alexi, but Miss Linden went on breezily, "All of us who watched the tumblers had sweets, like everyone at the fair. But the important thing is Cousin Anthony's ruby. I thought I lost it in—"

Sir Anthony turned again to Samara. "Have you heard of any other illness at the fair, Miss Connel?"

It was good of him to address her as a lady and she appreciated it. "I haven't heard. I could go back and ask around. It's barely dusk." She wanted to show him her gratitude for his gentlemanly treatment. It hadn't occurred to her that most people, certainly Miss Linden and Dr Halperin, would be shocked at her daring when she offered to go about the village at night. Even Sir Anthony might find it unladylike.

However, he surprised her by his attitude. What shocked him was not her daring to walk about unaccompanied at night, but that a lady would be asked to behave in this fashion.

"Certainly not," Sir Anthony said in a businesslike manner. "I will escort Miss Connel to the fair and locate the ruby earring." He added on a peculiar little sardonic note, "Not necessarily beside her bon-bons and wine. In fact, we may begin there and have done with bon-bons and what-not. You've no objection, Miss Connel?"

So that was it. All the charm, the gallantry, concealed a real interest, or suspicion, that it was she who had made his ward ill, whether she had stolen her ruby earring or not. Perhaps he had suspected her all along, remembering her remarks to Dilys about travelling to the Continent. Did he also believe she was willing to help those two young fools?

"I have no objection in the least."

He smiled. "Dilys, give Miss Connel your cloak."

"That won't be necessary," Samara said coldly. But Dilys took her heavy blue cloak with its three collars and threw it around Samara's shoulders, giggling at the fact that it was several inches too short for Samara.

"Of course," she joked, "if I keep eating those bon-bons and that wine, I may shrink even more."

Samara stared at her. There was an uncomfortable

silence before Sir Anthony said sharply, "That is not amusing, Dilys. I suggest you apologise to Miss Connel."

Dilys was quick to obey. But she added, still finding the subject amusing, "Don't look at me like that, Samara. You frighten me. Do you cast spells, by any chance?"

Dr Halperin cleared his throat.

"It may be coming on for rain by the time you return, Sir Anthony. Could this wait until the morrow?"

"Impossible," Samara said crisply, ready to forget the entire affair. "The band will be on its way tomorrow at dawn. They spend the night packing away what remains unsold or traded."

Sir Anthony unexpectedly found this attractive.

"A delightful life. It would suit me to perfection. So we must go tonight. Dilys, what is to become of you while we wander about looking for lost rubies and unpalatable food?"

Dr Halperin was firm about the solution. "I believe, in the circumstances, the only possible answer is for Miss Linden to remain in this office, as comfortable as may be. Perhaps in that large chair. It is well upholstered and I am sure she will be feeling more herself when you return."

For an instant the girl seemed disappointed and started to object, but looked at Samara and shrugged.

"I thought I would go to bed in one of those quaint bedchambers with the parlour, all above the tavern. Such a lovely name: Black Dog Tavern. I adore it."

"We only intended to use those rooms while we remained in the village this morning," Sir Anthony reminded her. "You seem to forget we have a coach and team returning to take us on our way."

Whatever Sir Anthony's plan, the one look Dilys had given Samara made the gypsy suspect the girl wanted to use the time she was alone to see Alexi again. He might be waiting above the tavern now. Samara was glad she herself was not given the task of watching over this volatile and dishonest creature.

While Dr Halperin watched them silently, Sir Anthony took her arm and strolled out into the street with her, remarking that they had the good fortune to be having this little adventure before torrents of rain fell on the God-forsaken countryside.

Whatever the complaints, it struck Samara that he was enjoying the unpleasant task under dark and windy skies. There was also the fact that her stride could match his, unlike that of the women he probably knew with their mincing steps and bodies bound by stays.

Dilys Linden's coat was something less than comfortable. Narrow across the shoulders and short enough to qualify as a pelisse. It wasn't the first time she had dressed with no thought for the changeful weather, but it was one of the few times when she would have liked to look her best in the company of a male.

Before they reached the fairground they could hear the Romany dogs clamouring for their meal, and amid this chorus came the deep, warning growl of a less friendly dog. Through this commotion Sir Anthony

36

noted with interest that some of the fairground visitors remained, drinking what they could afford of the whisky from over the border.

"They are still here. A hardy lot, your people," Sir Anthony told Samara.

She laughed. "Only half mine. I hardly know what I am. I feel Romany, but sometimes—"

"You are Irish."

"Just so. How could you know that?"

"Like you, I read the Tarot cards."

She felt a little better about what lay ahead. He must have been interested in her or he wouldn't have questioned Dr Halperin about her. Not that this interest would save her if he suspected she was guilty, but at least it was something on her side.

Several women remained, chiefly trying to coax their men away from the last trading on the horse show, and the Spanish gypsy tumbler on the high rope.

But many of the gypsies squatted in little groups, separated by sex, as they ate their roast lamb and fish over small, carefully controlled fires and wiped their hands, shining richly with grease, on their arms for health's sake.

Having identified Samara to each other, most of them pursued their supper, went on gossiping about the day in their own Romany language.

Sir Anthony sniffed the delicious scent wafting toward them as they passed.

"Did you live like that?" he asked.

"Until I was five, and it tasted as good as it smelled."

"I've no doubt. Somehow, it never tasted like that in the Peninsula. We choked on most of it, sure that every mouthful would be accompanied by a dagger thrust from some lurking Spaniard or a few stabs from some Frenchie's sword."

She pointed to his left.

"I have the use of that wagon on occasions like this. The lantern in front will give you light."

He hadn't even pretended to look elsewhere for the earring. But if it had been lost here, then it must be here now. He would be apologetic when he discovered it.

He led her gallantly over a pile of properties, all rolled in a threadbare rug, owned by one of Stefan's cousins who expected to use the wagon when she finished with it tonight. Sir Anthony was going to examine it but she explained that it had been thrown there after she had left to tell fortunes with the Tarot cards this afternoon.

He was looking over her wagon, apparently studying it as a place to live. She watched him, asking after a minute or two, "Well, sir, have you considered joining the band?"

He looked at her over his shoulder. "Do you accept lodgers?"

Refusing to acknowledge that he might mean something more personal, she took this as an honest question.

"Not Gentiles – Christians. However, you might prove you are their true and dependable *gadjo*. Every band has one."

He slapped the side of the wagon in a quick gesture, then held his hand out to her for the key, asking at the same time, "I suspect a *gadjo* is someone who helps you out of difficulties with – what? Magistrates? Or Justices of the Peace?"

Ignoring that, she warned him, "The key turns hard. The lock is a trifle rusty." She handed him the key, then took the lantern off a hook over the roof to raise it high. He had opened the door but he looked back. She swung the lantern over the ground, illuminating corners and little pools of darkness on the gravel with, here and there, a flattening of the moorland grass.

He stepped back down to the ground and examined the shadows more carefully. It was soon obvious to both of them that the earring was not there.

"I was a fool to let her wear the damned things but she begged so much, nothing else would satisfy her. I expect her mother promised that if she was a good girl, she would inherit the entire set. It's what they call a parure, you know. The necklace, a circlet for the hair, and a bracelet."

Worth a fortune. Even the stone from one earring would provide a handy little income.

He finally lost interest in the ground and threw the door open. She followed him in. The crowded little room was stuffy, as he noticed at once.

"Is it always this warm in here?"

"Sometimes we are grateful. It becomes fairly chilled as you go further north."

"Yes. I can see how—" He took the lantern and raised it to illuminate everything in sight. It was unlikely the earring would have fallen elsewhere, unless it had been deliberately concealed.

She was desperately anxious to find the jewel and knelt to feel the floor but found only a needle someone had lost at once time or another.

Sir Anthony moved to the other end of the wagon and also knelt to trace anything else on the floor. Since she hadn't taken out all of her property the interior was dusty, dirty and strewn here and there with a bead from some costume.

As he moved back toward Samara, who was reaching under an ancient bonnet box that had belonged to her grandmother, he suddenly exclaimed, "Ah!"

She looked up. From under the edge of the cot where Dilys had sat, he drew out a little string of braided blue silk thread.

He examined it but there was no need. Anyone could see that whatever it had been attached to was missing.

"What would you make of that?" he asked, dangling the braided threads before her eyes.

He knew perfectly well what she must say.

"It seems to have held an ear-bob." She looked up into his eyes calmly. "An ear-bob which is missing. At the moment."

Five

" It certainly isn't here." He was smiling but she found that smile all too knowing.

She tried to conceal both panic and fury.

"You seem pleased, as though you knew what would be found, or not found, as the case may be."

He set the lantern on the floor and was rummaging about, shaking blankets on the cot and looking on the floor for whatever might have been concealed in their folds.

"Please, she begged him haughtily, "I'd rather not be suffocated by all this dust."

Despite her objections, she examined everything he turned aside, but she felt that it was time wasted. In all likelihood, either Miss Linden, or more likely Alexi, had made away with the jewel for reasons she could guess at. Very possibly to finance the absurd romantic flight to the Continent.

Sir Anthony turned up some more trivia and wiped his hands to free them of dust and she asked finally, "If the ear-bob wasn't lost by accident, do you believe I am responsible?"

He stood up, brushing off his heretofore spotless

greatcoat and admitted, "No . . ." He looked at her in that pause, making her exceedingly uncomfortable. "But I think you know who has it."

It was frighteningly close to the truth. She could only remain firm in her story.

"I think Miss Linden will find it shortly, lost in her clothing. The jewel fell off, was caught in her coat or her gown."

He reached out to her, making her recoil a little. Amused, yet annoyed, he said, "Stand still. I am not about to undress you. That happens to be the coat my little cousin wore when she was in your wagon."

Feeling ridiculous, she patted the bosom and skirt of her gown, and then realised that with beads and coins sewn to the material the earring might be caught anywhere.

"The coat," he pointed out and put an arm around her shoulder, removing the coat. He spread it out between them, feeling the lining.

"Try the sleeve," she suggested.

He gave up. She had lost that little way out of the problem. He hung the coat back over her shoulders, remarking as his arm warmed her shoulders, "We must try this once again, when we lose an earring."

He could make a jest even now when she was being accused of high theft, a deadly crime. She wished she could be sure he was interested enough in her to realise there was no proof of her guilt except circumstantial evidence.

She tried to shrug him off and was surprised when he resisted her effort and then let her go of his own accord. She was not used to men she couldn't control. He broke what had become a pregnant silence. "Now, what are we to do? Report this business, of course. But do you imagine we will accomplish anything if we force all your friends to submit to a search?"

She had recovered her poise and was relieved that he treated it, or pretended to treat it, lightheartedly.

"Somehow, I feel we would be wasting our time, sir. But I am willing to gamble my future and my life on another method."

"You interest me. Are you about to offer me your quite remarkable self in exchange?"

She jeered. "What? Something you would regard as of little worth? No, indeed. But there are those in Marika's band who do find me worth more. If they think I am about to be punished for someone else's crime."

He stared at her, frowning, as though he expected to read her mind. He seemed astonished by her offer.

"Are you sincere?"

"Certainly. Don't you believe in loyalty among friends?"

"I do not. I am almost tempted to accept your offer just to prove you are wrong. My cynicism against your belief in your fellow men."

"In a sense, I am their *gadjo*. They will not let me suffer for something they could cure so easily."

"Easily? How?"

"Come with me to Marika or Stefan. They will put out the word to everyone in the band."

He shook his head. "I wish you were a wagering woman."

Then he helped her down off the steps of the wagon. She said, "Follow me." He kept an arm under hers and did not let her manage to get ahead of him.

She felt an exhilaration at the prospect of showing him there was loyalty among her people.

In spite of the rustling around of those who were beginning belatedly to pack, including the rattle of harnesses and the loading of the wagons, most of the gypsies turned to watch Samara and the outsider who accompanied her.

Seeing Sir Anthony's fascination with this outdoor life, even on such a wretched night, she pointed out various details.

He said wryly, "It is attractive to me, but I have slept outside on many occasions, especially in Spain, and if I were to choose, I would say, give me shelter in weather like this, and preferably no enemies with knives hiding behind every bush."

"Was it really so bad?" she asked, genuinely interested in what he felt about the war and his part in it.

A pair of men passed him, knocking his hat off with a roll of carpet. He made no objections as he picked up the hat, shook the damp off it, and placed it carelessly on the back of his head. He looked after the labourers to see what they were about. Their lengthy black hair almost blinded them to the crowded movement ahead. Then, as he saw her amusement, he said, "I think they need more army discipline."

He thought this over and added, "But not in ours. Now I think of it, there were times when their discipline would have been exemplary to us. Maybe Boney could have handled them."

She had always been fascinated by the Corsican but thought she would do better not to bring up that subject now.

As it was, she secretly marvelled to realise that in the last few minutes she had almost buried her fears of the future.

She faced them now as she saw Marika's solid form ahead of her, directing several of the women who were trying to control their rough team of horses, heavy with winter hair.

He found something of more interest when she called his attention to a single female managing a bored and stubborn bullock. The girl, probably all of eighteen, had not changed from her costume fringed with gold pieces. She was very pretty and her dark eyes shone as she saw Sir Anthony pass her.

He marvelled at the strength of these people and when Samara merely smiled rather sardonically, he said, "Their lives are not easy, are they?"

"They have one thing before all else."

"Oh? What could that be?"

"They have freedom. They belong to no one. They are older than you and your kind. They follow no law but their own."

"Even though it may lead them to prison for life? Or transporting to the Antipodes? Or . . ."

She looked at him. "Or hanging? Yes. Even then."

"As a magistrate I wonder how I would regard such a plea. You would be up before our laws, not yours."

She dismissed this as though it had nothing whatever to do with her.

"Fortunately, the honour of my people is greater than you are used to. Here we are." Marika had turned, hearing their voices, and Samara signalled to her.

"Interesting," he said. "I will be able to hear just how you manage this."

Her smile was tigerish. "Just so." She surprised Sir Anthony by presenting him to Marika. It did not happen to him often that a gentleman in his position was presented to 'a wild gypsy', but he behaved with commendable manners.

The two women used a Romany, language which was totally unfamiliar to him and he was at first disappointed. Then he became interested in trying to figure out from their inflexions whether the woman would actually help Samara.

Samara explained succinctly and described Miss Dilys Linden. Marika looked puzzled, then glanced at Sir Anthony and repeated some words, including a male name that sounded like 'Alex' or 'Alexi', which she questioned.

Samara reminded her in English, "It is of great importance. Sir Anthony is taking me to our local Justice of the Peace, the magistrate of this area."

"When?" Marika asked in a tense voice.

"Tomorrow," Sir Anthony said in his coldest judgmental tone.

The two women looked at each other. Marika's voice was unexpectedly lower. "I will see if it is so. If it is, it will be done."

Her worry was contagious. If, as Samara suspected, the theft had been arranged between Dilys and Marika's son, it was quite possible the boy had grown away from his people. His loyalty, and perhaps passion, would put Dilys before his mother.

But she saw Sir Anthony looking at her and she knew he was not surprised. He had known all along how it would be. All her talk of loyalty among people was a dream.

"Come, sir," she ordered the man she now considered her jailor. "I've done all I can. You are in command now."

He took her arm. It had been a dashing, polite gesture before. Now it was the magistrate whose hand closed on her as they walked toward the entrance which had now been knocked down and was being stored.

Marika called after them suddenly.

"What shall be done with your property, Samara?"

Sir Anthony looked over his shoulder. "I'll send someone for it."

Efficient, of course. As she might have expected.

They were on the cobbled street again where the last human shouting, the weird sounds of animals coughing, blowing and bawling began to fade, and Samara asked her companion directly, "What am I accused of? You can't say I stole your cousin's jewel. She simply lost it."

"Probably."

She wondered if he was joking. It was hard to tell.

"Then how can you really charge me with high theft?"

This time she thought his eyes smiled, though his lips remained businesslike and firm.

"I believe the earring was stolen. I think you know who took it."

It was not very satisfactory, and it showed a cruelty that put her on her guard again. He knew a gypsy would have little chance in a court of law.

"And if I run away in the night? Or are you leaving in ten minutes?"

"No. We won't leave until tomorrow."

She glanced at him and then quickly away. He was watching her with interest and went on, "You won't cheat me. I have laid a wager on you, and Tattersall's will tell you I usually win. Besides, it might be difficult for you to leave this wild neighbourhood with no coaches passing in the night."

"Nonsense. I could take some coins off my petticoat and make hire of some transportation in the village. A gig. Or even a curvicle. A horse. A mule, if necessary."

He laughed. "Must I take your petticoats hostage?"

It was all a joke. It must be. Meanwhile, he talked to her as if he considered her a female of the streets and no better than she should be. It was a daunting idea. Nothing romantic about it. But at the moment she had little choice.

"This is my grandmother's house, and just in time," she told him as a slap of wind buffeted them and lashed her hair wildly across her face. Before she could do anything about it, he raised his hand and brushed the clinging strands away from her eyes.

A Splash of Rubies

Ironically enough, for an instant she thought this aristocratic stranger, who had never seen her before this morning, would lower his head and kiss her. She drew back an inch or two, more surprised than shocked, and when he raised his head again without touching her, she was disappointed. This time she was truly shocked by her own reaction. She moistened her lips but turned, with his fingers still fastened around her arm, and unlocked the door which was squeezed between two bay windows.

There were no outward indications that the little house was her place of business; that customers, mostly female and young, came here for love potions, business predictions, readings of the Tarot, and of course, the inevitable reading of the crystal ball. That could only be guessed by peering into the windows.

He put out his arm, holding the door open for her, and looked over her head at the crystal ball in its glass container, looking like a low-burning coal in the swinging lamp of the street.

"Have you seen your future in that?" he asked.

Her dark eyebrows raised. "It is murky at this point," and he seemed amused, as so many of her reactions amused him.

"May I go in now?" she asked. "Or will you have a guard posted?"

"We will see." This time, as he let her go, he pinched the bridge of her nose and reminded her, "We've a wager between us. No witchcraft, with you turning to dust and vanishing."

She taunted him, "This wind is turning to rain. You

49

had best hurry back to the Black Dog Tavern, unused as you are to our climate."

He did not bid her goodbye but started off, holding his hat. At the corner, where the street branched off and one side plunged down the hillside, he looked back at her but made no signal. Then he went on up the hilly main street, the tails of his greatcoat and collars fluttering around him.

She went inside. The little house suited her life. It contained one room which was built and furnished around the fireplace where she prepared her meals with the help of hanging pots, pans, double vessels for gentler heating, an oven beside the hearth and numerous equipment formerly employed for other purposes.

The crystal ball was set on the old, scarred gaming table which still looked elegant when polished. The table was near one of the windows, the only object that could be seen clearly from outside the house. A couch which was little more than a military cot occupied a good part of one wall, along with a painting of an Irish tinker's wagon-house which had been her birthplace and her first childhood memory.

Her grandmother, a governess with excellent credentials, had despised her son's mode of living and blamed it entirely on his gypsy wife, but when the older woman died, the drawing of the wagon had gone up on Samara's wall.

There remained little else to Samara's house except an additional room that had once been a shed but was now her scullery, being sufficiently cold to preserve her food for a few days.

An outhouse, at a short distance down the slope, was used by several sheepmen when they came into the village from the moorland. No villager lived in the deserted little house next door to her. None had ever lived there since her grandmother's death. She was aware, without caring, that the villagers were uneasy about living close to 'one of them as made terms with the devil'.

She looked around while shaking off the coat that belonged to Dilys Linden, and smiled grimly. Would she be accused of stealing the coat as well?

She liked the tight little place. Her real world, aside from the work that gave her a livelihood, was the moors and there was nothing tight or little about them.

She warmed her hands at the coals of the fire. Though they still glowed black and scarlet, they were almost ash, and she stirred them up. While she stood there she looked around at her small haven. It was comfortable because the world of her imagination was outside these walls and belonged to her.

What if she were locked away for ever? Her tormentor had hinted that her crime was high theft and the minimum punishment she could expect for that, especially considering her gypsy blood, was the rest of her life in some cell. It would be smaller and certainly less comfortable than the room she was in now.

A living hell for anyone whose life was the out-of-doors.

She went to the far wall, uncovered newly hanging garments freshly washed and pressed, a shift, a pair of petticoats, a blouse and skirt.

A few gold coins were sewn in the skirt and silver in

the inner petticoat. This would be enough to keep her for some time, together with the Tarot cards and her own wits.

Best to take a second skirt, the fine golden-tan velvet, in case the less expensive skirt became stained. She hadn't decided yet whether to wait for Sir Anthony's decision, or Marika's possible rescue, or simply to start out now in the night, carrying the bundle wrapped in her old shawl.

She would be capable of walking to a village beyond any where the magistrate might pursue her, and from there, hire a mount of some kind. Or a gig and a strong mare. She could reach the coast and certainly pay the transportation either on a lugger bound for the Irish Sea, or somewhere on the Continent.

She thought with a certain triumph: the Linden child is not the only one who may escape to the Continent. Samara knew she would certainly find some of her own Romany bands somewhere between Genoa and the Kingdom of the Two Sicilies.

While her thoughts twisted and turned and she remained undecided, Samara considered all the important objections to an escape and while doing so, glimpsed her figure in the mirror beside the painting of her parents' wagon. The sight of the flamboyant and theatrical gypsy costume reminded her that she would be tracked down from the moment she left Heaton Clough.

She would certainly need the heavy cloak she wore in midwinter. That must cover the bright clothing she normally wore. That and one of the old shawls over her head, of course.

She hadn't cleaned the dripping pan under the fireplace spit last night as she intended and the room still held the odour of the bit of lamb she had roasted. It would certainly give Sir Anthony Linden an unpleasant opinion of her to take away from here.

But if she were taken away forcibly? Or if she were gone when Sir Anthony and someone from the Justice of the Peace arrived? She wondered why she should care if she was already halfway to the coast when Sir Anthony entered the little house. It surprised her that she should be concerned for his opinion of her as a female and not as a criminal.

How would it matter if she was never to see him again?

She knew the sooner she left the village the more chance she had. She certainly must be gone while it was still dark.

She changed hurriedly and then took the coins out of the clothing she had worn at the fair. No time to sew them into her travel cloak and it would be more difficult to stride along at her usual pace with that encumbrance. She tore off the extra coins and dropped them into the reticule suspended on long drawstrings from her neck.

She went to the door, opened it, and was slapped in the face by the windy mist. It was partly this and partly her sudden realisation that Marika had never failed her which stopped her now.

She counted on her suspicion that Alexi had taken the ruby earring. He might have persuaded Dilys Linden they would sell it and use the proceeds to run away. Knowing Alexi, Samara had no doubt it was a lie. He probably intended to keep the jewel and eventually abandon the girl.

Marika would find that out almost immediately. But would Marika risking involving her son with the courts and the inevitable result for a gypsy? Or would she find a way to save her son and Samara?

She had based all her hopes on Marika before Sir Anthony alarmed her into thinking about running away. To remain here would be a gamble. She looked across the room at the worn set of Tarot cards she always used at home. It was kept for those visitors who came in to the little 'Witch's House' as the children of Heaton Clough often called it.

She took up the cards, asking herself: Shall I go now and hope to escape that devil of a magistrate? Or shall I put my trust in Marika? Let us start with trust in Marika.

In dealing out the long columns she saw dangers, passionate signs she seldom found, and one card that spun to the thinly carpeted floor. She kicked it over with her shoe. The Hanged Man.

The next fortune the cards told was definitely negative and the card she feared was very close. Satisfied that the first reading was her answer, she felt that her destiny had been written for her in the Tarot deck.

She settled back in her chair, yawned, and waited for the morning.

Six

S amara slept comfortably.

On warm nights, unusual in this part of the world, she often slept out on the moors, with the small moorland creatures attending to their own affairs. There would be nothing beneath her except one of her father's cloaks in which she was wrapped, and a bundled shawl under her head.

She was never disturbed by strangers, or by villagers, many of whom, she knew well, were afraid of her 'evil eye'. Only an occasional sheep, having lost its flock and its bad-tempered but faithful dog, might wander up and whiffer in the gypsy's ear. Then, having felt Samara's pat and her well-remembered voice, the disturber would be off across the moors.

With the exception of one or two sheep dogs none of the animal life troubled her. And only the human beings were uneasy when they encountered her. This made her smile when she noticed it.

But tonight, as it verged into morning, she was awakened by a human hand across her eyes. Not a villager's. One of her own kind.

The hand was removed. Could it be Marika? Only

she and a few other gypsies were likely to come
unbidden, through the usually unlocked utility door
which opened out upon the hillside and the outhouse
nearby. Only the gypsy band found that this place held
no terrors.

She opened her eyes. The wind had gone down and
was succeeded by the pre-dawn breeze, but the lamp at
the turn in the two streets was still alight, though it
might be knocked off its hook at any time.

Leaning over her she made out Alexi's young face
with its brass-gold complexion, but his mouth lacked
the usual smirking grin. It was, or seemed to be,
trembling with fright.

She asked calmly, "Have you the jewel with you,
Alexi?"

He moistened his lips. Though he made a point of
speaking English in public to please the young females,
he spoke in his parents' original European tongue
now.

"I had to. She said if I had it when they searched the
grounds out there, we'd lose our chance to escape from
that guardian of hers. The jewel isn't his anyway, you
know. It was meant to be hers."

"Really? I was of the impression he had simply
permitted her to wear it."

"Oh, one of his lies, I expect. But it would give me
deadly trouble if they found it on me. Or on my – the
young lady who loves me."

"And do you love her?"

"Of course. We are going to be together always. But
we can't do anything without selling the earring and

the other – and whatever estates belong to her legally. Poor little thing. How they take advantage of her!"

He added hopefully, "It's just a matter of time. We took her earring too quickly. It should be done when he no longer suspects. Dilys knows a solicitor. He could be very useful. In Bath where she is to attend a Young Ladies Academy after she completes her schooling at Sir Anthony's home in Rye. That's on the Sussex coast."

"And how do I enter your plot?"

His spirits were rising. "Don't you see? Sir Anthony likes you. You must say you found the jewel. Then he won't pursue this business of searching the grounds where we held the horse fair."

However many times he fooled his parents, he seldom succeeded in convincing Samara of his innocence. Perhaps that was why he feared her.

"You do see, don't you?" he went on anxiously. "It's the only way, now that he knows it's somewhere about here."

Her scorn came through in her quiet response. "One thing only we agree upon. The earring must be returned at once. Permanently."

"Oh, but soon, we will need—"

"Permanently."

His hand went to the sash under his sheepskin jerkin. She smiled. He hesitated, bit his lips. He was still afraid of her, even when armed against her. Then he complained, "You don't know what love is. She looks at me. I can't help myself. She is clever, too. She has ideas. We could go so far, if only . . ." He became humble, begging again, the knife in his sash forgotten. "We would pay you back . . ." He looked around nervously. "What's that?"

"The street lamp. It throws shadows across the window."

One thing was evident. She knew she had to get the earring back to its owner, as she imagined Sir Anthony to be. If it disappeared again, there was all of the Continent in which it could be swallowed up, besides providing these conniving children with the money to live in what would undoubtedly be a life and a world of crime.

She got up. "Come. We'll have done with this matter now."

He was still protesting when she opened the front door and took his arm. "But we must have the ruby later, when my darling is sixteen. Only a few months away . . ."

Almost unconsciously, he was fingering his sash but she tightened her hand on his arm. She scarcely gave a thought to the possibility that he meant anything serious by his knife threats. He was by nature a coward and she was a strong woman.

"Now, listen to me," she ordered in a voice he had never been able to argue with. "We will go behind the street buildings here, past the churchyard and into the grounds where the horse fair took place. We will be together and I will look about, with you beside me. In the area where the animal dung has not been cleaned yet. We must hurry."

"Not—" He wrinkled his nose. "But that's a vile smell."

A *Splash of Rubies*

"Certainly. Where else would a magistrate and his aides fail to look?"

Alexi stared at her and then had to stifle his laugh. "Only you would think of that, Samara. Let's hurry."

They passed the turn in the street and he followed her behind the abandoned little house above hers. She felt that thus far no one on the main street who happened to be out at this ungodly hour would notice them on the path that passed close upon the edge of the hilly downward sweep into the valley.

In a minute they passed a path that crossed the cobbled main street, very near the Black Dog Tavern. Samara glanced over at the parlour room above the tavern, noting that a lamp was lighted and burning low enough to set it smoking in faint trails across the uncovered window.

Sir Anthony must be up. Or could it be Miss Linden? She doubted that, unless the girl was trying to see whether Samara had agreed to the plan worked out by Alexi and herself. The earring would be returned, but by Samara. Alexi and Dilys would not be concerned in it and later, perhaps in a matter of months, or even weeks, the two would-be lovers would resume their romantic and thieving plan, escaping to the Continent.

It was a plan worthy of children, but worked out so carefully; only Samara would be at fault if Sir Anthony had already notified the local Justice of the Peace. Of one thing Samara was certain: the little jewel must be returned and the sooner the better. After that, its protection would be strictly in the hands of Sir Anthony.

59

It was just on sunrise when Samara and Alexi reached the much trodden grounds where the gypsy band had held their horse fair. The morning appeared to be bright with a sky swept clear and crisply blue. Having dealt with the village authorities to whom they made their usually moderate payment, the band had left the area in fair condition except for the cow-dung, horse manure, and other leavings of the livestock.

Alexi held back, complaining, "Can't we tell the magistrate we've seen the earring shining in the sunlight but we haven't touched it, for some reason? Afraid to? Too valuable? That sort of thing."

She said firmly, "Come!"

He dragged along a few feet behind her until they came across the grass, which had been fairly stamped into the ground.

Several horses had been tethered at the end of this area. It was still some yards from the front of the wagon that, through long custom, had been used by Samara.

It would serve. The Linden child might easily have lost her earring early in the day, while walking near the wagon, waiting for Samara's arrival.

She had not done so, as Samara knew very well, but it would seem plausible to the local authorities whose jurisdiction included Heaton Clough.

Alexi looked down, kicked the drying clods of dung and manure with his sandal, and muttered, "I wouldn't touch that with my own bare flesh. I just couldn't!"

Samara took a bright, flame-coloured kerchief out of her skirt pocket and spread it in her palm.

"Just put the earring in the centre here and cover it with dung."

"But I tell you, I—"

She shook her head at his delicacy, then reached over, scooped up enough drying horse dung to cover the shining little jewel and stood up.

"Now, you may go."

He felt her contempt, but was too anxious to be off and far away. He had no time to take offence.

She watched him go, then expressed her own feelings as she spat on the ground into the dung pile. She folded the kerchief over the jewel and tied the four corners. Then she started back to the street. Alexi was already running across the graveyard which separated the parsonage from the Black Dog Tavern. She smiled grimly.

The light in the upstairs parlour of the tavern was out now, which was not surprising. The air was bright with sunlight and the breezy blue heavens had been swept clean.

Alexi was out of sight and she felt herself very much alone amid the gravestones which had everywhere fallen flat over sunken graves. Some of the stones were cracked or broken across, and spring tufts of grass were beginning to shoot up between the broken slabs.

She found Christian burials unpleasant. They reminded her of her cold, intellectual grandmother, who had tried but failed to find anything admirable in the gypsy's daughter.

She crossed the graveyard to the rear door of the Black Dog Tavern, and went inside the passage, which led straight ahead to the taproom off to one side, where an ancient staircase led to the floor above.

At that moment she was startled by a hand closing around her wrist in the semi-darkness.

She had made it a habit long ago never to let the villagers think they could frighten her. In a half-annoyed, half-amused voice, she ordered, "Stand out of my way. I have business with your guest."

"Oh? A pleasant surprise," Sir Anthony said. He acted quite as though he always seized hold of strange women in sculleries at dawn. "You've come to ask for more time?"

When she stiffened with resentment he added, as if the idea were out of all reason, "Or . . . now, don't make me believe you've returned my jewel."

"I've no concern with what you believe, sir. A problem has arisen."

"You feel a reward is due?"

She raised her chin. "I cannot accept the word of a stranger on such a matter. I should like a receipt to signify that I have found and returned this bauble."

He ignored her remark that his word wasn't acceptable.

"Bauble? How proud we are!"

He drew her out through the graveyard door again and leaned back against one of the few gravestones still standing. She made no effort to resist his treatment. It was wiser not to make trouble until she tested his mood. He seemed to be teasing her. He looked into her eyes and she stared back. She was not shy and never had been.

A Splash of Rubies

"Did you really decide to return it?"

"I really found it ten minutes ago. Whether I return it to you depends on whether I receive your written assurance that it has been given to you."

"You have it with you?"

"You have your personal card with you?"

He laughed and confessed, "I am defeated. Let me fetch up my card here. I have it somewhere on me." He made a performance of searching, which made her smile in spite of herself, especially when he offered the card to her, and assured her it would admit her to his home at Royal Rye in Sussex.

"Well now, I've done my part. What trick have you to play on me?"

She handed the kerchief to him by the four tied corners. He looked at it in his hand, studied her, and remarked, "A big packet for one small earring."

He probably still believed she was planning a trick against him.

"I gave the matter some thought last night. This morning I found it on the ground."

Obviously suspicious, he still seemed to enjoy their game. He gave no indication that he thought it might be deadly.

"Well, let us see if there is something inside that may bite us."

She said, "It was embedded, as you will see."

"See?" he repeated. "Smell would be more correct."

She said nothing but watched him untie the scarf. Once opened it exuded something of the odour remaining from the nearly dried dung. By now he must have guessed the origin of the smell but looked in as though the ruby stone, stained and unpleasantly odorous, was exactly what he had expected fo find. He poked the earring out of its nest of horse dung, sniffed it and began to laugh.

She did not join him. Fascinating as she found him, she was remembering all the misery and dread she had endured during what he may have considered a jest of the first order. Had he always known she was innocent?

He was still amused, holding the earring up to the light and watching the sunlight flicker off the stained ruby when his young ward opened a window of the Black Dog's upper floor and called down to the churchyard: "Did you find it, Cousin Anthony?"

He moved away from the tombstone, took a few steps forward, and waved the earring at her.

Samara took this opportunity to retreat to the churchyard gate, then started up the hill to the moors again. All the excitement and tension was over. She would not go up before the Assizes, spend her life in prison, or be transported in chains overseas.

There had been moments, however, when she enjoyed the dangerous episode. For the first time in her life, she had known what she thought of as a romantic escape. She had found Anthony Linden very nearly irresistible, though she would not dream of letting him know. They had nothing in common except a sensuous excitement, which was childish. She had enjoyed brief love affairs on occasion, but nothing in her life had ever made her believe there could be a relationship of any consequence between herself and the Christian world of her grandmother.

She might have wished Sir Anthony hadn't been detained by his chattering ward at the window above the tavern, but it was probably just as well.

No matter. At least, she was still able to live in the free, unfettered world she had known all her life and was quite sure she couldn't live without.

As she passed the area occupied on the previous day by the horse fair, she noticed several youths in sheepskin jerkins clearing away the debris. Driven by the enthusiastic vicar of the local church, the youths concentrated on removing the animal debris first, but she knew they would be searching for anything lost at the fair or any trinkets that pickpockets might have left for a later rescue.

She started on the rocky high road to Leeds, then cut across the wide, rolling moorland and began a climb over the heath from whose heights she would eventually see the major area of the West Riding with its occasional stone boundaries and its look of a grass eternity.

At the summit of the next green wave she stopped and removed her cloak as she looked ahead of her, down to a dell carved out long ago by a tiny stream. There were a few straggling trees outlining the path of the stream and indicating a pothole further along where the unwary might be sucked down, and where sheep were lost now and again in the foggy bottoms.

She did not go down to the stream yet but stretched out her arms and breathed in the cool, spring-scented air. It held a glorious feeling of freedom and limitless space.

She was still standing there with her arms spread, surveying the primeval world before her when she realised with some resentment that she was not alone. She swung around and tried not to show surprise that Sir Anthony Linden had approached across the hilltop and was now within a few yards of her.

She took her arms down, demanding in her amused way, "What else is missing, sir? Am I to be searched out here where I have no defence?"

He laughed at this. "You, with no defence? I've no doubt you would shoot me between the eyes if I so much as—" He hesitated, added unexpectedly, "—if I kissed you goodbye."

Her left hand moved slowly over the folds of her sash, around to the back. She wondered what he would do if she brought out her sharp, shining Toledo dagger.

"Do you care to try me?"

He held up both hands in surrender.

"Far from it. I really do want merely to say goodbye. And to remind you that we are having a village fair in Rye within a fortnight, and we badly need a teller of fortunes." He looked down into her eyes, an experience not common to her among the stocky sheepmen.

"What?" she jeered. "And this time an entire set of jewels vanishes under my nimble fingers?"

He reached out, took a strand of her wild, windblown hair and rubbed it between his thumb and forefinger. She was intensely aware of his touch, so close to her cheek.

He told her, "We will lock up all the jewels. Ah! That is better. You can laugh."

His hand tightened suddenly on a handful of her hair and before she could react, he had pulled her head close. His mouth, which had been in her thoughts more than she would like to admit, was hot on her lips.

Imprisoned against his body by force and wincing at the painful pulling of her hair, she kicked him. It was a kick blunted by her skirt and petticoats, and when she failed to free her arms, trapped against his hardened body, she resorted to her last weapon. She knew she had responded warmly to his kiss but when she freed her mouth her strong, white teeth bit his lip.

The fact that she had felt a passionate response heretofore unknown to her had nothing to do with her reaction. She was unused to being handled with a force very like her own nature. She too had a primitive streak that had obssessed her for a few seconds.

She stepped back, her eyes narrowed as she watched his reaction. She saw that his flash of anger had vanished as he stared at her. His fingers touched the reddened spot on his lower lip.

She reached into her useful sash and drew out another kerchief, this one much smaller and made from a hemmed bit of muslin.

"Use this."

He used the muslin and grinned.

"I see you can draw blood."

"To remember me by."

But he recognised a fellow spirit and did not show anger.

"Well then, will you come to Rye and tell fortunes, for the Old Seamen's Fund?"

She pretended to consider. The truth was, she had no desire to travel so far from her own world.

"You tempt me, sir."

"Well then?"

She felt an unexpected excitement at the look in his dark eyes. "Let us see what the cards advise. If there are enough jewels to make it worth my while, who knows? I may make the journey."

He took up her fingers, slapped them lightly and almost before she was ready for goodbyes, he turned and strode away across the moor grass.

Seven

S amara found the days after the departure of the gypsy caravan unusually monotonous. Most of the young women of Heaton Clough had spent their meagre shillings and pence at the horse fair and in the following days only a handful came to hear their fortunes, watch Samara read the many-hued glass crystal and predict their future from the Tarot deck.

She spent a surprising number of hours recalling Anthony Linden.

The weather having suddenly turned spring-like, he specially crept into her thoughts when she walked the moors. Sometimes she pictured that rolling vastness as the wild grey English Channel off the coast of Rye, Sir Anthony's town, scarcely more than a village along the Sussex coast.

Travelling through the countryside, so foreign to her own world, would certainly have been one of those adventures her ancestors had enjoyed.

But she had never really considered travelling the length of England without the tribe she had belonged to all her life. Her family, in fact. And she knew too that in many of the counties she would not be permitted to remain, possible not even to enter.

Certainly, the cities would present enormous barriers to her, dismissing her, like all gypsies, as a 'vagabond', one of those criminals to be driven out by dogs, staves and guns, unless, as a troupe of fairground entertainers, they had one of the hard-to-get permits. This meant a great deal of bargaining and a price, often in gold.

She doubted if she could fool anyone into thinking she was a Christian, and in any case, her pride would not let her make the attempt.

It wasn't that she had such a passion to see Sir Anthony and his conniving little witch of a ward. Not at all, she told herself. But quite suddenly the world had opened out like an enormous picture beyond her reach. Was the recent episode what the world outside had to offer?

She would never be happy in that world. She was sure of that. But a brief taste, and then home again to the moors . . . It would make her appreciate her own life all the more.

No use in thinking of it, however, unless she found a family of gypsies with whom to travel. And she wasn't at all sure she would enjoy living so close to a band whose members were strangers.

But the days that followed offered very little joy and excitement, until one morning on the threshold of spring.

Her particular talents had not prospered since the horse fair, probably because too much had been spent with Stefan and Marika's band. But this morning two teenage girls had come to have their palms read and ended by becoming intrigued by what they thought they saw in the crystal ball.

As usual, the attractions of a young sheep farmer in the valley town of Horsley had sent them scurrying to discover from Samara which of them would succeed in winning the sheepman's attentions.

Samara was amused and gave them an equivocal answer which suited them both. The cleverest and gentlest of them would win. The girls, laughing at their private thoughts, went out assuring each other that, "It'll be you, Gussie . . . No. It must be you . . .", each girl certain that she herself was far more modest and certainly more clever than the other.

Having satisfied them, Samara began to line her petticoats with a coin here and there, wondering at the same time what would ever give her pleasure enough to make the spending of coins in this village worthwhile. She would have done better to leave with Marika and Stefan and the others.

Less than an hour after the two girls went away happy with the future predicted for them in the crystal ball, Samara was visited by two of the village women: the baker's wife and the sister of the local curate.

Since neither woman had been in her house before except to collect for the factory child labourers, Samara needed no crystal ball to tell her this was trouble. She quickly hid her sewing and the coins under her couch-cover and went to the door.

71

She was polite and cool, knowing that her worst mistake would be an eager attitude. Long ago she had learned that they all regarded her friendly efforts to ingratiate herself as the prelude to a theft.

They were here to warn her away from their children. They looked at each other and the buxom baker's wife, feeling herself nudged by her companion, began.

"We'd as lief you wouldn't be reading my girl's fortune. It's 'gainst the Good Book."

"Which you'd not be knowing," put in the curate's little, pale-eyed sister.

Clearly, the baker's wife felt her companion wasn't putting quite enough force into the order.

"Raisin' spirits from the dark, it is, girl. Bringing sin to the children and naught a word of truth passin' your lips."

"It's only a toy," Samara said with a faint smile. "If they are not yet intelligent enough to understand games, they may have their money back. Sixpence for the reading or a shilling for all of it, the crystal and Tarot and their palm reading."

The two women looked at each other. The curate's sister rubbed her hands on her reasonably clean pinafore.

"We'd be much obliged if you'd take your witchcraft from our two girls."

The baker's wife burst out, "There's some as heard you'd gone and took the ear-bob from the magistrate's ward. Not that we believe them. We've naught to say when you deal with others, so don't you be putting a curse to me and mine."

Samara studied them, wondering if they had already gone to the law. They backed away under her gaze. Clearly, they still thought she was a witch.

"What can you say against me? My father was Irish, and his mother and father were Irish."

The baker's wife girded herself up to tell Samara hoarsely, "The Justice of the Peace may say you're a vagabond. All your kind are. You lay hands to my Susan again and I'll have you turned out of the parish for a worshipper of the devil."

"Ay. And—" the other began, only to have the door slammed in her face. The women shrieked. The door had just missed the creature's nose.

Inside the house Samara grinned. There was always something ominous and frightening about her grin – her teeth were seen at their best!

Outside, the baker's wife called to her, "You leave our children be, and we'll do the same by you."

The two women turned and marched back up the street.

The petticoat Samara had been working on fell from her couch. She picked it up and bundled it in her hands, tearing at the bright, heavy material. But then she laughed at her fruitless task. "You are like me. Too tough to destroy."

She smoothed out the petticoat, realising that she would very probably be thrown out of the county if they reported her to the local magistrates.

Then she wondered. Was this a sign?

She reached for the cards and laid them out in columns on the bed. Very soon she was calm, concentrating on what she read in the colourful deck. There was no mistaking the message.

Movement. Travel. Trouble. No mistaking that. Stains of what? Blood? No. Jewels. Rubies. It might be rubies. But there were lucky signs. Then blood (or rubies?). Then luck again.

Two messages came clearly: Either rubies or blood, or both. And movement. Travel.

She shuffled the cards again. They appeared in different alignment, yet the message was almost the same, except that a clear sign of romance was closer.

She shuffled the cards impatiently and then threw them back on the little table.

Was she really in danger of being ordered out of Heaton Clough?

Moving suddenly, she got out her best red knitted shawl, threw it around her shoulders, and went out upon the street. The little insular world looked very much as it always did, with many of the village men in the fields below, the sheepmen on the moors above, and the women going about their business, paying no attention to her except for sideways glances, once or twice a nod, and sometimes a whisper and a nudge to another female.

She might have one friend here. She walked up the hill towards Dr Halperin's office, taking the long strides that put her ahead of everyone she passed. There was less wind than usual but the breeze played about her lengthy, somewhat unkempt hair, occasionally brushing tangled strands across her forehead and her high-boned cheeks.

Dr Halperin was just returning from a visit to the Upworth child, whose father owned the Black Dog Tavern. He looked tired but he was obviously glad to see her.

"Not ill, I trust, Miss Samara?"

"Not with any ailment you can cure, Doctor."

"Well, let us see about that."

He opened the door for her and gallantly ushered her into the dark interior.

While she stood there, considering what she would tell him, if she had actually come to him for advice, he threw open the shutters, explaining that the child he had attended would be up and about in a matter of hours, perhaps less.

"Poor child! She was trying to imitate the tumblers she saw at the gypsy horse fair. Fell on her left arm. But she is a girl with stamina. Like you, Miss Samara, if you will forgive me."

She nodded. Her brief smile told him nothing. Whether she was flattered or offended would be impossible to say.

He offered her his most comfortable chair and asked if he could fetch her a mug of something. "That is to say, a glass."

"I'd take your good advice and be much obliged," she told him as she sat down.

His eyebrows raised. He seemed nervous, anxious to please her, and ventured, "I have a little brandy. I know some of you – I mean, your friends – prefer wine, but—"

"I only want your advice, Doctor."

"Oh, yes. To be sure." He pulled a ladder-backed chair nearer to her and sat down on its edge as if ready to spring up at any minute. "But not about your health, you say?"

"No. Only indirectly. Tell me, Doctor . . ." He assumed his authoritative, medical look. "You hear all the gossip hereabouts."

"Possibly."

"Is there a plan afoot to have me certified as a vagabond and ordered out of the parish?"

He hesitated, biting his lip for an instant.

"Not precisely. There was some talk among a few of the females in the village – mothers of susceptible girls, you know. But it was voted down for . . . for the present. You've nothing to fear, so long as you don't accept money from children under sixteen."

She reminded him grimly, "That is to say, the girls who are my greatest admirers."

"Oh, I wouldn't say that." He was playing the kindly physician. "All it needs is a little discretion on your part."

Discretion! Her people had roamed the earth longer than these pale creatures who issued all the orders. And now they were strangers on their own ground.

She said, "There are occasional bands related to my own people who came over from the Continent between the wars. They are here in the country now. One of them needs someone who understands the crystal ball and can dance. I thought I might join them for the spring months if I like them. They have permits from the locals in several Midland counties."

"Oh, but the danger. You may be jailed. And if you are alone – if you don't care for these people – you are in great danger." He was agitated, which amused her. He was too shy to demonstrate any interest in her – absurd as she found him – but still he wished her to remain here.

No matter. It would avail him nothing. She had little understanding of the gentle and timid. Bad enough if they were female but even more futile if they were male.

Unable to remain seated, she got up and walked to the window whose view encompassed a high section of the distant moor. Could she be happy elsewhere? Even for a short time?

Not happy. She did not ask for happiness in the sense that the silly girls reading the crystal prayed for it.

Experience. Excitement. A passion for life.

She realised suddenly that she had long missed the passion for life which should have gone with her feelings as she crossed the moors into a life beyond that of her humdrum neighbors.

She swung around.

"I have felt, Doctor. But I have never lived what I feel."

Dr Halperin protested, "But my dear Samara, you cannot live the wild life of your ancestors. This is England. Every Englishman will be your enemy. The very dogs in the street and on the chase would tear you to pieces."

With the realisation that she finally knew what she

wanted, Samara laughed. She was not going to let these possibilities turn her from her course.

"You are right. I may not like the new band. First, I will make my way to the Sussex coast. There is an old smugglers' town called Royal Rye. If I don't find my life there, I will go to the Continent, or to the West Country. My own people make their homes with their wagons on the Dorset Heath."

He shuddered. "A horrible life. You will abandon your grandmother's world entirely."

"It has abandoned me."

The doctor raised his hands and began to pace up and down before he turned to more practical matters.

"Well then, you must take precautions. Forgive me, but your style of dress, your hair, all these touches of your past must be forgotten."

"Of course." She had watched him pace and now teased him. "And if I dance, I shall wear a staid and proper gown such as the instructors at the female academies wear. I shall be a perfect lady and no one will be the wiser. At least Grandmother's teachings wouldn't be wasted."

He recognised her teasing and shook his head in despair. "If you did, you would be safer."

"But I would not be myself."

He tried another path. "It will cost you money. Even you cannot walk all the way. And if they see you as you are now, even the mail coach will not accept you."

She gave that some thought and nodded. "Someone else must buy my ticket."

"Yes. If you have that, they may not make difficulties. I can obtain the ticket. The coach will take you to Nottingham. From there you would fetch up eventually in London. I came by that route myself. Unless you prefer to stop over. But that might bring trouble, with the lodging houses refusing admission."

"There is that," she murmured thoughtfully. Then she dismissed the problem with a wave of her hand. "But I daresay a few shillings will make the difference."

"I wish you would not do this mad thing. At least wait until another band that you know comes by."

But she was already on her way to the street door with the parting news: "I won't promise to become one of the females I see around me. I wash more often than they do, and I do not wear their ugly gowns and shoes. Except in rainy weather."

He followed her uncertainly, sighing over his vain efforts at teaching cleanliness. "How very right you are. We should all be healthier if the females, not to mention the males who won't even let me treat them, would abide by a few sensible habits."

She asked, "Do I meet your requirements, Doctor?"

He was no longer shocked by her frankness. "Very much so, Miss Samara. I could wish your gypsy friends would learn from you. They are worse than the locals."

She did not argue with him. It was pointless, but she smiled. "Put the blame for my habits upon my grandmother. What a creature she was for that horrid soap she made, and the water. The water was never hot enough. I nearly froze. But I prefer it to the saturated perfume and spices of the baker's wife."

"Ah, true enough. Spices overlay but do not conceal."

She stopped in the doorway.

"May I count upon you to have me put on the waybill of today's coach?"

"What? This very afternoon?" He reached out as if to stop her but was afraid to argue with that steely determination of hers.

"If you will not change your mind."

"Wise man. You know me. I will present myself as respectably as may be, and your responsibility is ended."

After a moment's reluctance he ventured: "You are probably aware that Sir Anthony Linden has a manor house somewhere on the marshes near the town of Rye. Since he is the Justice of the Peace in that area, you may call upon him at need."

"Call upon him?" she scoffed. "When he accused me of stealing that child's ear-bob?"

"He told me you had found and returned it."

So he knew about that.

He added, "That was the morning his carriage left. He asked where he could find you."

"Oh?" She was pleased that he had gone to so much trouble, in spite of the kiss – or perhaps because of it.

"And you directed him up there to the moors?"

"I didn't think you would object."

She shrugged and opened her reticule to get out the fare for her journey.

He wanted very much to say that her place on the waybill would be his farewell to her for the next few months, but he hadn't the money laid by for such a gesture, and in any case he wasn't sure how to broach the matter. She might believe he had some ulterior motive.

She gave him the silver. Whatever she thought, he saw her smile as she went out into the street.

Eight

S amara's wardrobe had been simple enough when she travelled with Marika and Stefan's band, a wardrobe of costumes appropriate to her role. The less valuable of them were worn every day in Heaton Clough. But apart from occasional trips to Leeds and York to restore certain parts of her wardrobe, clothing meant little to Samara. In the winter she wore a heavy black wool cape, and in other seasons one of her grandmother's prized possessions, a close-fitting, high-collared crimson coat that had belonged to her father.

She packed the necessities for her performances in her grandmother's old portmanteau, wore one of her less-adorned, full-skirted wool gowns for the journey and made a fairly neat bundle of petticoats, shifts and shawls, which she tied with a sash.

She locked her door and walked up the street to wait at the village fountain with her portmanteau in one hand and her bundle of clothing swinging from the other. She regretted having to wear her seldom-used crimson bonnet but it was necessary. No comb would get through her long, unruly hair without a struggle.

She was the object of considerable interest to the townspeople. Several of the females with whom she had a reasonable relationship nodded to her and a sheepman's two sisters asked where she was bound.

"To see the world," she told them easily, as though she undertook this sort of journey every month.

The ladies exchanged glances, more puzzled than unpleasantly curious.

"I envy you, Samara," the younger of the two told her, and her sister agreed as they walked on. Perhaps they were kinder than she had thought – or they were relieved to be rid of her.

Samara set her luggage down to await the arrival of the rackety, swaying coach and team while she looked after the two women and wondered why they couldn't go out to see the world if they chose. It wasn't the expense. She herself earned no more. But when she wished to do a thing she did it. Gentiles were strange in many ways.

Curious people. They took so little of what life offered. Their attitude, however, doubled her excitement at her own decision.

Soon the noisy tearing up of the dirt road across the moors by the coach and team reminded her that the little adventure was about to begin. At the same time Dr Halperin came out of his office and crossed the street to join her.

He was polite but still a little worried.

"I trust there will be no problems on your journey." He glanced at two of the local women who had turned back momentarily. Heads together, they exchanged opinions as they went on, leaving the doctor even more cautious.

"Please do take care, Miss Samara. Speak to no one on the coach. Mind your property, your reticule."

She grinned. "This to me, Doctor? With all the thieving talents of my ancestors?"

He was forced to laugh but insisted, "You cannot trust strangers. Especially travellers. Ah! Here it comes."

He stepped back behind the slowly dripping fountain as the coach and team came to an abrupt halt beyond it. Several bored faces, male and female, looked out as the grizzled coachman opened the door and let down the steps.

Dr Halperin surrendered Samara's tickets to be checked on the waybill, then he offered Samara his hand and, to his embarrassment, she leaned out of the open door and kissed his somewhat worn cheek.

"Thank you, good friend."

He blushed fire-red, to the amusement of the other passengers, and Samara sank back against the tattered squabs of the corner seat after noting that her luggage had been taken around the coach and thrown into the boot.

The carriage was yanked forward, backward, and then the team was on its way, led carefully down the cobbled street by the elderly coachman.

Samara looked around at her companions, aware at the same time of noisy conflict overhead, which told her that the coach roof held some unruly passengers. She wondered what it would be like to enjoy the invigorating wind in her face, her hair flying around her like Medusa's snakes, and the heretofore unseen world everywhere in sight.

It was a long time since her childhood arrival in her grandmother's village Then she had slept in a rocking corner of the mail coach, missing some of the excitement as she and her grandmother changed coaches and she was urged to stop fidgeting, stop trying to look out at the passing scene when they stopped, and above all, to be silent.

She remembered how humiliated and angry her grandmother had been when someone remarked, "What strange eyes the child has! Look as though they'd see through you! What sort of creature has such dark eyes?"

She had long ago discovered that she was the object of much interest to her fellow travellers, who did not hesitate to say her darkness was that of a 'witch or a gypsy baggage, capable of casting a spell'.

She soon saw now that in spite of her dull clothing, she had already aroused suspicions of her background. Though the two elderly males studied her face in a furtive way, the women had their heads together as they talked in sibilant whispers. They were looking at the hem of Samara's coat, or perhaps at her sandals.

The sandals, of course.

She did not own any of the ugly woollen or worsted stockings worn by most women. It took considerable willpower to avoid drawing her sandals back and covering them with her coat hem, but she did not move for a minute.

Then, quite deliberately, she crossed her legs at the knee. This brought an audible gasp, though she displayed nothing but her ankles. She settled her head back, bonnet and all, against the soiled cushions behind her, and thought about her future plans, providing she was permitted to entertain at the medieval coast town of Royal Rye. A great deal depended upon whatever help she could obtain from Sir Anthony. Had he remembered her parting behaviour? That bite had been one of her best. But it might very well have tantalised him. At all events, he must take her as he found her. She suspected he knew that.

The buzz of the women went on but not loud enough to be audible to the men in the coach. One of them went to sleep, punctuated by snores, and the other, somewhat older, with dirty whiskers around his mouth, unlike the clean-shaven style in fashion for past decades, sat staring at her while his tongue travelled around his lips. She found him more amusing than disgusting.

One by one, her companions went off to sleep as the lowering sun began to cast long shadows across the road ahead. Samara was surprised to find she was too interested in the landscape itself, which exchanged forbidding moorland for early blooming plants, rushes and wandering brooks.

So many ideal places where a gypsy troupe might find a haven for themselves. She must remind Stefan and Marika of these places to make camp for the night. It occurred to her unexpectedly that the eternal charm of the moors had a rival in the many delights of the lowlands.

When they reached the valley town of Keelty, where the people of her village often traded and some of the children were set to work at the valley factories, the two male travellers got down and went their way while the females remaining on board exchanged their opinions of the departed rider.

"Filthy fellow," One of the women noted of the bearded man. "Dirty as a gypsy."

The other hissed a warning and both glanced at Samara who returned their nervous stare with one of her toothy smiles. What cowards these creatures were!

Minutes later the next passengers climbed aboard. Leading them was a young man in a sheepskin jerkin with two pockets. Samara straightened slowly as she saw the slit pocket in the tail of his jerkin. It was an old trick and she was ready for him.

He took the middle seat next to her, followed by a stout woman with a basket of eggs, who took the remaining seat beside the young man in the jerkin. A boy of three or four scampered up, put the basket of eggs on the young man's lap and sat down on the fat woman's lap. Before the young man could continue to play this little game with Samara on his right, she took the basket, reached over him and put the basket back in its original spot. in the boy's hands. The child looked surprised but grinned at her. She grinned back. The ladies across the aisle watched some curiosity. Probably thought gypsies ate little children, she thought sardonically.

The young man seemed closer to her than she had noted when he entered the coach. If, as she thought possible, he really was a cut-purse or pickpocket, she wondered how he would manage with everyone's eye upon him.

A scrawny male came hurrying out of the Keelty Ordinary, wiping his thin lips on the sleeve of his green redingote, and waving to the coachman. The latter had been discussing the breed of the lead horse with a raw-boned young ostler and broke off to put the steps down again for the newcomer.

With the waybill amenities over in a moment as the sun disappeared, leaving only hazy rays of light, the impatient fellow in green hopped into the coach interior, which smelled of bodily warmth, and made himself comfortable beside the two chattering women.

Obviously, he didn't like the look of Samara and blinked as if he didn't believe what he saw. She stared him out of countenance and he gave up the unequal contest, but he kept sneaking little glances at her for the next hour. It was not a flattering observation.

Eventually, in her boredom, she tried to guess when the young thief beside her would make his move. Someone in the coach, probably the newcomer, had eaten heavily of garlic at his afternoon dinner. The odour spread through the coach and the ladies exchanged frowns and significant signs of disapproval.

Samara usually enjoyed mealtimes when travelling with the gypsy band. She thought there was nothing like the rich, hearty smell of lamb or mutton cooking over fires under the trees and beside a faintly gurgling brook. But she could imagine the shock and revulsion of the two women here if they saw the males of the band enthusiastically rubbing their bare, dark arms with the succulent meat grease which every gypsy knew was good for the skin.

She dozed off into a half-sleep in which she was still aware of what went on around her. Presently, a small movement along her thigh, which she felt through her gown and her heavily decorated petticoat, made her aware that her young male neighbour had slipped his hand down between their bodies, probably aiming for her reticule, which had slipped to one side of her lap. She remained still. The hand moved several inches along her thigh. Suddenly, the young man jumped and inhaled with a hiss, between his teeth. His hand looked red across the back of the palm where the flesh was thin.

At his movement the woman beside him looked surprised. Her child awakened from a nap to announce that he was hungry. His mother hushed him, distracting attention away from Samara's neighbour who had attracted whispers from the two women in the seats facing him. They probably suspected the fellow was annoying Samara in quite a different way.

The young would-be thief behaved respectably until the coach pulled up in the coachyard of an Ordinary and everyone but the sleeping man in the opposite corner got out for a late supper while the ostler and the coachman discussed the roads ahead.

The thief did not follow the others to the inn but hung about the coachman. Samara wondered if his effort to obtain her reticule was not a result of his profession but his shortness of money. He was obviously an amateur.

When Samara returned to the coachyard after finishing her quick meal of mutton and eggs, she gave the old coachman a faint smile, taking care not to overdo her friendliness.

The two chattering women had already been helped into the coach when Samara reached the steps.

Suddenly the coachman's gruff voice called out, "Not in this carriage. You!"

Taken unaware, she thought he must be speaking to a newcomer behind her and started up the steps, but then his gnarled fingers tightened around her wrist.

"We've no need for you gypsy thieves. Off with you!"

She was taller than the grizzled little coachman and was tempted to make a quarrel of it. However, the coachyard was filled with passengers climbing down from the big northbound mail coach nearby and in the end, as Dr Halperin had predicted, she could not win. In various towns there were laws against 'vagabonds' and she did not feel inclined to fight them all at this time of night.

She stepped back and raised her voice to let the passengers of both coaches hear her. "The man who told you that about me – the young man leaving the yard over there – is the real thief here. The ladies on our coach will tell you, it was that man who tried to rob me. I used my fingernail upon the back of his hand. Ask him to show his hand to you."

The women in the coach stuck their heads out of the door and for an instant Samara thought they were going to defend her. But one of the women called nervously to the coachman, "Can't we get on? My family is expecting me. You must know Squire Tillotson of Newbegin Hall? Your next stop."

Samara waited with a show of firmness but her hope of aid was gone. She knew that nothing she could say or do would be as persuasive as the magic name of some unknown Squire Tillotson, whoever he might be.

"You have my property in the boot, sir. That and the waybill should tell you I belong in that carriage."

Apparently, he had expected her to speak in some kind of doggerel, because he gave her an odd look. He glanced around toward the mail coach and its scramble of travellers going to the inn just as the last of the male group headed toward the coach roof of the southbound coach making its way out across the yard.

The young thief who had obviously accused her was mingling with the mail coach and its northbound passengers. He must expect better fortune on the mail coach. An idea occurred to Samara.

Would there be time?

She became indignant but kept her voice low-pitched in spite of the depth which sometimes made hearers uneasy.

"I'll wager you a new silver piece that sly rogue is your thief."

The coachman looked around again, saw there was too much commotion in the coachyard for anyone to hear.

"A silver piece says you're lying, Mistress Gypsy!"

He stalked a few lengths across the yard, finding Samara beside him when he reached the young thief who was already in the impatient line waiting to reach the mail coach steps.

There was a slight touch of danger in what Samara hoped to do, but that sort of danger merely stimulated her. As the coachman abruptly stopped the young man, Samara moved around him, insisting, "I felt his hand, impudent dog. Ask the ladies opposite me. They saw him. He accuses me now to be rid of me." She backed away, past the flustered coachman. "Disgusting creature! Ask him what he stole from the passengers."

"Well now, this gentleman—"

She took a chance. "Ask the ladies in your coach. They saw him."

One of the ladies who had whispered through the young man's furtive efforts to steal Samara's reticule had already come down the steps. She moved toward the coachman despite the objections of her talkative companion. She bustled a little and was obviously unused to this public display.

Several other passengers and one of the two ostlers joined the group, everyone expressing an opinion. Samara had not hoped for much from the woman who had come from the coach but she was pleasantly surprised when the woman suggested in a modest but firm voice that the young man be searched.

The young man was indignant and ready to challenge Samara when the woman who had remained in the coach leaned out and called, "Amanda, we are late now. Do come along."

But the coachman had been moved to settle this

matter in a hurry. He pulled at his whiskers and reached out to seize the young man's jerkin.

"Sir, let's be seeing them pockets. Then you can go."

While the young man struggled, a fact that put his audience against him, the coachman, assisted by the ostler, put his fingers into the slit pickets at the front of the fellow's jerkin. They came up empty. Samara began to wonder if she would have to call their attention to the rear pocket when the ostler called out, "How now! Here's a little sommat."

He reached two fingers into the back slit pocket and came up with Samara's thin copper wrist-chain that several of the women in the crowd pointed out as similar to the gypsy woman's other jewels.

"It matches her ring. The wristlet belong to that female."

Samara cried with horror, "My chain! My chain! My precious husband's gift."

As she spoke she clutched her throat with the hand that wore a small garnet stone with a copper setting. Her dark eyes glittered with tears. "A souvenir of my dead husband."

The females present were shocked and moved away from the accused who was babbling his innocence while wondering just how it had gotten into his pocket. Samara was at first surprised that he did not accuse her of putting it there but realised that somewhere on his person were probably other stolen items from another coach, items which Samara was not responsible for having placed there.

She appreciated his position but since she had been

his first victim, she had no sympathy for him in spite of her own guilt in his present problem. He should have known better than to involve her in his goings-on.

She remained tearful until she was politely helped back into the coach and the woman across the aisle from her muttered to her friend, 'I do hope our troubles are now over. Heaven knows, it is time."

Samara silently agreed with her.

Nine

Having made her way down from Nottingham to London, sleeping in her seat when the swaying, jolting mail coach permitted the luxury, Samara found her luck holding. Her place in the coach was not questioned again, although she was aware, with both amusement and disdain, that other riders left space between 'the gypsy woman' and themselves.

She expected little of London and was not disappointed. She had no use for cities, and this great capital seemed typical, full of noise, crowds and coal dust.

Carrying her bundle of costumes and her portmanteau, she entered the public room of the densely crowded inn to wait for the mail coach which would serve her purpose. Bound for Hastings and the south coast the coach would pass the Romney Marshes, and Royal Rye on its hilltop.

She knew she would have to take the Rye–Hastings mail coach which passed the Romney Marshes somewhere or other before she reached Rye, but surely the coachman would know where to set her down so that she might walk to the coast. There was bound to be excitement and lights, torches, lamps and the usual ribbons and pennons wherever there was a gypsy carnival.

As she passed the open taproom doors she suddenly knew her luck was in. A large black cat, trailed by five kittens, stalked in front of Samara toward the tapster's bar near the doors. At the end of the bar the cat curled up comfortably while her kittens squirmed and edged their way beneath her.

Even before Samara saw the badly misspelled placard on the wall above the bar, her confidence grew. Number five was her lucky number and a black cat had always been the best of omens to her.

She strained a little to read the announcement informing all travellers that a gypsy carnival was entertaining above the Romney Marshes near Rye. There would be games, gypsy dances, drawings, prizes, *and other usual entertainment*. The last words were underscored. This had to be the carnival of Sir Anthony's half-joking invitation.

Thanks to the black cat and her kittens!

An hour or so later in the day the northbound mail coach began to make up for the tiresome journey to the border and travellers pushed their way into the taproom for quick ale, beer, and even quicker refreshments.

Apparently, gypsies were not a common sight in the city and since the Gentiles bored her with their curiosity and sometimes their arrogant remarks, Samara followed the decision of the cat and her kittens who untangled themselves and stalked toward the inn yard. Samara lifted her property and went out of

98

doors. There was action here too, so she moved to the area near the high road in the shadows that followed on a blinding sunset.

The high road was noisy with the passage of several marketers' carts in which eight men and women and two half-naked children were crowded, all but the children with their hands bound behind them. The men were standing, one of them blubbering. Another leaned over the cart's side crying to the curious crowd: "It's innercent I be, ma'am . . . Never done nuthin'. That I'll swear to."

Samara was caught by the snort of a man beside the complainer. His eyes were fringed with heavy lashes, black as midnight. The evening breeze blew his uncombed curly hair as wildly as Samara's did on the moorland heights.

A gypsy.

Others in the carts, seeing her sudden attention, called to her as well. Two were gypsies. When she turned to the others, the nearest gypsy stared at her but gave no sign of kinship. She understood that.

Obviously the carts were full of prisoners bound for questioning, or even sentencing, and if they were found guilty, they faced the Assizes or more closely, London's Newgate and what came after.

The carts had stopped, the ostlers were busy attending to the animals and several people in the inn yard, hearing hoofbeats and the rattle of a curricle, pointed to the dashing vehicle coming up behind the carts. The curricle swung around them and the man at the reins, obviously an aristocrat, called a greeting to one of the ostlers who returned the greeting with a salute.

Samara was shocked to realise she knew that speeding rider. As the curricle rattled onward and out of sight, the ostler said to his companion, "He has a fair way of handling those beasts, has Tony Linden. Small wonder them Frenchies was beat."

Samara felt sick for a moment. She had been fooling herself, trying to believe that his cruelty and teasing had all been his idea of a jest. But beneath all that humour and charm was this creature who really could send men, and women, to the gallows or the ends of the earth in a hell ship for minor crimes, and in the case of her own people, with little or no evidence.

Around her she became aware of the usual excitement among the coaches pulling to and from the yard. She must decide what to do. She had no desire to return the way she had come, back to her grandmother's little cottage in Heaton Clough, at least not until she had seen more of the world.

There were strange, exotic areas still unknown to her, the duchies and republics of Italy, the little kingdoms and Papal States. They were still a challenge in many ways, as they had been three or four hundred years ago when they were briefly, at least, her ancestors' home as they wandered Europe.

Just as she felt now, her Romany bands had never been satisfied in one place, nor were their Gentile 'hosts'.

She smiled ironically, remembering the teachings of her mother's gypsy ancestors who practised theft and purse-cutting at an early age. But they left killing to others, remembering only to keep as their friend one *gadjo* in each area whom they would never harm and who would protect their band at need.

I should have remained what I was, she thought. Count upon none but my own people and our own *gadjo*, whoever he might be.

Otherwise, there might be no law to defend her, as there was none to protect the people she saw today.

At the same time, if she kept travelling, there would soon be an end to the silver pieces she had collected. She would have to resort to the thefts taught her in her babyhood. But even if she was not guilty, the law would still be her enemy.

One hope occurred to her.

The noble Justice of the Peace did not know how her feelings had turned against him. Let him believe she still trusted him. If, indeed, he had ever believed that.

She was awakened to the present by the calling of the southbound coach from London on the High Road, bound for Rye and Hastings. At the same time there was a traffic problem at the south entrance to the innyard as a familiar curricle returned toward the inn where the team, behaving with great presence of mind, pulled up short and Samara saw Sir Anthony swing out with a grace that attracted comment from the crowd.

An ostler took his horses. The magistrate asked him something and upon receiving a nod and a few words strode off into the crowd toward the inn. Samara watched him until he was out of sight. She wondered why he would be stopping at this public inn. This was not nearly so important as the question of what her own reaction would be if he came to see her at the carnival.

It was only thanks to young Alexi, who feared her influence with his parents, that she had escaped riding to trial in a cart with her hands bound behind her, like the unfortunates she had seen minutes ago. She owed Sir Anthony nothing. Even his kiss had been forced upon her. He could hardly blame her for that, but her few dealings with him showed him to be a ruthless man whose word could send her to Newgate Prison or to the nameless horrors of a prison ship bound for the Antipodes.

She heard the southbound coach called again after the blast of a tuneless horn and she moved out of the shadows towards it. Something like a dozen passengers rustled across the yard dragging their luggage which was removed and stowed in the boot. She followed, hurrying a little to avoid finding no seat left.

Suddenly an arm shot across her breast, stopping her mid-step. A teasing voice spoke close to her left ear.

"Where in the devil's name were you? We've been on the look for you since yesterday."

"Who told you I was coming? No one knew except . . ."

But of course. Dr Halperin knew Sir Anthony. He was the only person who had learned exactly where she was bound. It was annoying. She had always been secretive and even went so far as to banish any temporary friend who violated her privacy.

He looked into her face. He was obviously in the best of moods and fully as attractive as she remembered. The delivery of prisoners to trial had not troubled his mood.

She wondered if he had given the slightest thought to to the hopeless cases of those bound prisoners. At Heaton Clough he had seemed to waste little thought on her fate, beyond the interest of a gamester in whether he or she would win his little private bet. And yet, there had been no clear evidence that she had stolen his ward's jewel.

She explained coolly, "I go where my work calls me."

He saw her teeth flash in the light of a swinging lantern and frowned. "You might be a witch when you look at me like that."

"You don't like women who smile?"

But he was more observant than she had thought. "Your eyes are strange. There is a light in them but no smile." He shrugged and motioned to one of the ostlers. Then he added to Samara, "I'll take you to the carnival. A friend of mine is concerned in it. An event for the Orphans Society she has organised. Will you join us?"

"Certainly. I am notoriously charitable."

This time he laughed at her sardonic tone. Her pride would not let her admit she had come here expecting to make money, not to give it away to a Christian charity.

The ostler brought up the team and the fragile curricle. Then he reached for Samara's luggage and the bundle of costumes. She was about to give him orders when she felt herself lifted off the pebbled ground and set on her sandalled feet in the little carriage. For a moment she found herself looking into Sir Anthony's eyes in confusion.

Slightly dazed by all this swinging around, she could only clutch the seat, trying to catch her breath. Few men either dared or were able to treat her so cavalierly. There was always a touch of danger about her that had served to protect her for several years.

Meanwhile, she noted that Sir Anthony was definitely amused as he got in beside her while the ostler threw her luggage in at their feet.

She had seldom let herself be found in this awkward position, where someone else might be amused by her confusion. As he busied himself giving the signal to his team and they left the yard at a spanking pace, she used the few moments to breathe deeply, control her stiffness, and look about her with nonchalant interest. Wanting very much to know what would happen next, she managed to conceal her uncertainty, and remark in the most casual way, "This gypsy carnival, as they call it hereabouts, what does your friend know about my people?"

"Who? Elaine?" He scoffed. "She knows nothing whatever about gypsies. But she fancies herself in the costumes your people wear." He looked at her. "I'll feed your vanity by telling you she won't do justice to them. But you must have seen that happen before."

She smiled without replying, and did not look at him, thought she was aware that he had not taken his eyes off her.

104

They were well on the high road now, finding themselves in the company of wagons, pony carts and an occasional coach with a giggling quartet of revellers.

Sir Anthony's team reached ahead, and he remarked with some interest, "Quite a crowd on the road. Off to the carnival, I'll be bound. The countess and her charity will be the talk of Brighton. Money always impresses Prinny."

She knew 'Prinny' was the Prince Regent, but what the countess had to do with the matter was beyond her. She repeated, "The countess?"

"Elaine, the Countess of Penryn. We were betrothed at birth. Tiresome custom, but it appears that even the Peninsular Wars couldn't separate us."

She had no reason whatever to be disappointed at this news, but suddenly, she found herself resenting his betrothed and hoping her carnival would fail. A woman of wealth, and title, betrothed to a more than ordinarily attractive male, was using Samara's talents for a charity in which Samara had no possible interest.

"Far be it from me to fail the Countess and her Christian charity."

He grinned and looked sideways at her. "You will be enthralled by the lady. Perfect manners. Superior intellect, and a golden beauty."

"I am dazzled already. Good manners are so uncommon these days."

"True. You are tantalised into kissing them and then they bite you."

She began to laugh, enjoying this exchange, and

105

aware that she was perfectly willing to take up the challenge. When she defeated Sir Anthony's pretensions, there would be the game against the Golden Countess of Penryn who apparently expected her to make this precious charity rich on her own fortune-telling.

The rest of the ride was surprisingly pleasant and it became evident, as they turned off the high road onto a sandy trail lined by thickets and early spring brush, that the carnival or charity was attracting half the coast.

Samara looked around with interest. He was caught by her careful observation.

"Why are you smiling?"

"I was just thinking how useful I might find this carnival as an idea for Marika and Stefan." She went on as innocently as possible to her nature, "For their charity, of course."

"Of course. Ah! There's the Golden Lady herself."

Samara, who had been enjoying herself, looked across the busy ground and saw a slender, fragile-looking female in a child's idea of gypsy garments that looked like wisps of delicate colour. She wore a beaded cap and her spun-gold hair puffed out around it.

"Lovely creature," Samara said smoothly. "All these years and you haven't married yet? You are very slow, Sir Anthony."

"Oh, well, the wars, you know."

She guessed he was enjoying himself, especially when it suddenly became clear he was trying to make her jealous.

"These unfortunate wars," she agreed. "They are responsible for so many delays . . . She sees us."

"Good. You will enjoy each other's company."

Samara could imagine how much she would enjoy this angelic creature, but she gave him a gentle, wholly artificial smile.

"How well you know women, Sir Anthony."

He was busy summoning the Countess of Penryn's stable boy and appeared not hear her.

Ten

The lamps swaying from long poles over the beach strand illuminated the hull of a wrecked lugger and several longboats pulled up to shore, and streams of light fluttered over the foamy shore.

None of it looked even vaguely like a gypsy camp, though sheep wagons had been pulled out from the sandy road to an area around a crackling fire. Evidently this was meant to suggest a gypsy gathering. The costumed visitors and the Countess of Penryn's aides moved about waving daggers, blunderbusses and an occasional sword, but not one instrument appeared as useful to Samara as the thin, dangerous knife in the sash of her gown under her cloak.

The beauty with the spun-gold hair gave an order to several men setting up lengthy tables obviously in the Gentile fashion, which Samara realised were meant to represent the diet of gypsies. Samara was amused to find men in wide-legged trousers and striped singlets, their stringy hair bound at the nape of their necks by stained ribbons or string.

In Samara's opinion they were more likely to be found smuggling brandy up the long strand of beach.

These were certainly not gypsies about to entertain the crowd that either watched them or laid down sixpence for Cornish pasties and ale, evidently meant as gypsy food.

With the golden hostess coming to welcome them, Samara started to swing herself down, but seeing Sir Anthony come around the carriage, she waited, for once behaving like a weak-limbed Gentile, until he lifted her down, taking his time before his two hands around her waist released her.

The Countess was now near enough to have a perfect view of Sir Anthony's conduct. Samara gave him a tantalising look and was rewarded by the effect of that look on her companion. He did not remove his hands from her waist for another moment. Then he released her but motioned to Samara with one hand.

"Elaine, here is your gypsy authority. She will help you put this absurd company into some kind of order and correct what I suspect are numerous errors."

The Countess pursed her lips. She was not as young as Samara had thought, and after examining Samara from head to foot, she scolded Sir Anthony, "You did not tell me our gypsy was so – impressive. If we had any real gypsies here they would lose their hearts to her." She offered her delicately-veined hand to Samara. "Welcome to our carnival."

Samara could not miss the hand but wondered if she was expected to put her lips to it and curtsy. Instead, she raised her own strong, dark fingers until they touched the Countess's fingertips and said, "I trust I may be—"

110

She got no further.

"How good of you to say so. Of course, you may be of service to us in our little charity."

Samara nodded, looking around with disapproval. "I see so many amateur touches here, but as I was about to say, I hope to be able to correct them."

The Countess blinked her pale lashes but changed the subject a little obviously. "Tony dear, our adorable Dilys has made me promise that you would bring her to the carnival. She seems very anxious."

"Probably wishes she might see that boy she met last month at York."

Was Alexi somewhere in the area? The girl would certainly be up to mischief if he was.

The Countess caught her breath theatrically.

"Not that dreadful, dirty little gypsy she told me about. Oh, Tony! We must not let her be persuaded to see him again."

Samara had no doubt the insult was introduced for her benefit but before she could reply in the same vein, Sir Anthony cut in coolly, "You mean that handsome young rascal? Perhaps we oldsters haven't such clear sight. You and I, my dear Elaine, must take care how we view the young people of today, or Samara's generation will laugh at us ancients."

The Countess drew in her breath sharply, gave the silent Samara a glance and dismissed the subject.

"Perhaps our friend Samara – you did say it was Samara, Tony dear? – will be so kind as to change into her gypsy garments and examine the area where she will work. After that, someone will show her around and she can make suggestions. I do hope we can all learn the trick of playing gypsy. How amusing it will be!"

She turned to Samara. "Let me show you—"

But Sir Anthony was already taking Samara's arm. "An excellent notion. Shall we be on our way, Miss Connel?"

Samara found his methods crude and blunt but was enjoying herself immensely and went along with him. She did not look back but his rudeness to his betrothed said very little for their long relationship. Still, she had seen Stefan strike Marika, and they loved each other. Not as she had pictured some imagined love in her life, but she could never see herself struck without answering in more deadly coin.

When he left Samara in one of the sheep wagons, she hurriedly shook out her costumes, thankful that the heavy embroidery of gold braid and thread, and same cheap, but flashing jewels, had kept the materials from badly wrinkling. There was a cracked mirror in the wagon and she removed her ugly bonnet to brush and comb her lengthy hair. It was a vanity of hers not to cover it in the general way with scarves and when she had renewed the black kohl on her eyelashes and slipped half a dozen bracelets on her brass-gold arms, she felt that she at least looked the part she played. Perhaps her only reality.

Several instrumentalists were playing fiddles near the tumblers exercising in the nearby surf. She wondered if these Gentiles really thought they sounded like gypsies, even in this dark fire-lit night. After a moment, without seeming to show any interest, she noted that a plain, modestly dressed woman, looking like a strict governess, was stooped over the steps of another sheep wagon appearing to look for something she had dropped.

The minute Samara turned away as if uninterested, she saw out of the corner of her eye that the woman was back at her work, watching. Obviously she had been assigned to report Samara's activities. Of course. They would never trust her, in spite of Sir Anthony's good offices.

Money. They would always believe she intended to steal some of their so-called charity profits. She went back into the wagon and searched the interior whose only lighting was one candle rapidly wearing down. She located several strips of paper which would be used later for some of the carnival entertainment. In an excellent hand, well inked, they all said 'Orphans' Charity, to be collected by The Countess of Penryn.' These were no doubt leftover labels for the Countess's assistants.

None had been issued to Samara. Perhaps they thought she would keep whatever she thought she could get away with. She hoped, but wasn't sure, that Sir Anthony was not a part of this. She took one of the labels and looked for a container of some sort. Finding none, she assumed this was another little clue against her honesty. If she poured money out of her reticule they might believe anything. But what was their purpose? No one had a reason to dislike her except perhaps, the Countess, who may well have grown tired of hearing Sir Anthony, and even Miss Linden speak of her, for good or ill.

What a disappointment for someone when she produced all their profits! How would they know exactly the amount she had taken? So, obviously, someone would be on the watch. What childish fools people like the Countess were! They had little experience with Samara and her kind.

She looked out of the tiny window. The woman was still there but had moved to a less exposed place to watch her. Would she follow Samara? It gave her an idea. She went out boldly, strolled along toward the beach, then away and up into a thicket past the dry sand. She turned back toward the busy, noisy crowd wandering around and spending money on food or drink near the Countess, who looked very busy among several male workers.

Meanwhile, Samara noted that the 'governess' had followed her until she was called by the Countess. They talked in low tones and Samara went on, looking as sinister as she had often been accused of behaving. Let them be afraid of her. They would not be the first. She considered taking some of their profits when she had been cleared of theft, but she couldn't decide whether she was willing to let Sir Anthony discover he had been right all the time.

Thus far, no one had approached her about the purpose of her presence here. She walked slowly back to the crowd near the Countess and gave some attention to the absurdly costumed citizens of the area strolling along. Children chased each other through the surf. There was excitement when she appeared and the youngsters pointed to her, some calling to each other, "It's a real one. A real and true gypsy."

Another boy yelled, "Hold tight to every farthing."

She grinned at that and started across the sand with her long, haughty stride. As she passed through the shadow of wagon someone hissed to her and then she heard the unmistakeable language of her people: "I'm here, Samara. Don't tell them. Please."

She stared into the shadows. "You fool! The magistrate of this area is Sir Anthony Linden. He will undoubtedly suspect your part in anything that happens here."

Alexi smiled winningly. "Oh, I don't think so." He put one hand into his sash and pulled out three shillings and a few smaller coins from a lawn kerchief. "See? This was only an hour's work."

She looked skyward in disgust. "You are an idiot. You will be the first to be taken. No one would mistake you for one of their sort."

He pushed his curly hair under his head scarf, looking absurdly confident.

"I'm only waiting for Miss Linden. She has plans for the future. She's sworn we will be safe."

"You deserve what is waiting for you. Get out of this place. Go up to London where you will be lost among thousands."

He looked around, but saw no danger. "Maybe. After I've talked to Dilys. I will soon be her lover. Then, when we are on our way, her bridegroom."

"You are likely to be her dead bridegroom. These

are dangerous times for our people. This country still believes we worked for the French Service in the late wars."

But he was already backing away, still confident. He waved to her as he vanished into the brushwood that bordered the upper area of the long strand of beach.

She hoped that he would be a trifle more careful than usual, but knowing Alexi, she could only prepare for his rescue, if possible. Of one thing she was positive. She could expect no help from Sir Anthony. She remembered too vividly the sight of the prisoners in the carts and the magistrate's apparent lack of interest in them. Alexi was the last person he would help.

She looked around but the woman spying on her was nowhere to be seen. Alexi had chosen a dark and hidden place for their meeting.

She reached under her heavy satin overskirt, took out her favourite deck of Tarot cards and studied them before going on. A male voice called to her and she stopped again. An elderly gentleman in the breeches, wig and double-breasted frock coat of at least a score of years ago hurried up behind her and enquired, "I believe I have been sent by the Countess of Penryn to find you. You have some eager patrons waiting for you. Might you not be—" He hesitated. "Are you the young lady who is telling fortunes tonight?"

"Quite true, sir. If you will point out to me the table and lamp I may use?"

"Oh, much better than that. You see the tent beyond that overturned lugger? It's really quite comfortable.

Two lamps for you to see your crystal better. We are fortunate to have you, a genuine— That is to say . . .''

"A genuine gypsy?" she echoed. "You need not be concerned. I assure you, I am genuine.''

He looked her over through his quizzing glass. "Happily so, ma'am. As I said, it's beyond the boat, yonder.''

Her dark eyes surveyed the boat. "A smuggler's boat, I've no doubt.''

He said hurriedly, "Ah, yes, ma'am. But I am persuaded a smuggler or two would never frighten you. That is to say . . .''

She smiled. "Quite so.''

He cleared his throat. "I had better tell the Countess I have carried out her instructions.'' He started past her, then halted briefly to remind her, "Ma'am, I understand you read cards too. You've been told about the fortune-telling?''

"Is it forbidden?''

"No, no. Nothing like that. In the circumstances, the more patrons you have, the better. But of course, you understand that.''

He went on his way back across the sands and up to where a crowd was gathering at the entrance to the flag-decked poles with their painted banner naming the charity sponsors.

Samara saw the cards in her palm and was about to put them away when she heard booted footsteps crunching the sand behind her.

Sir Anthony was coming with his ward Dilys. Samara looked around, trying not to make the movement obvious, but though she was relieved to see no signs of Alexi she felt that he had by no means left the beach. At least he was being cautious.

Dilys seemed friendly, considering her recent efforts to entangle Samara in the 'theft' of the ruby earring. Samara stared unsmiling at her, saw Dilys's wide-eyed, girlish smile and didn't believe it for a moment. But the girl seemed to be trying to tell her something and she suspected Dilys knew Alexi was here and wanted Samara to keep silence.

Samara remarked on a casual note of business, "You are here to have your palm read, sir? Or is it your pretty ward who would like the prediction of the cards?"

Looking relieved, the girl giggled and clutched Sir Anthony's arm. He was looking annoyed and certainly suspicious.

"Neither. Dilys, go and see if you may assist Elaine. She is looking for you."

The girl curtsied to Sir Anthony and hurried off. Samara noted that she glanced right and left as she ran, as if she were looking for someone. But her guardian did not see this. He was intent on getting to the subject that evidently occupied him. As Samara turned her attention to him, his strong, hard features softened, and he surprised her by smiling.

"What a nuisance that girl is! But now, shall we proceed to our business?"

"I was told to go about and demonstrate a gypsy's life and be certain everything was accurate. However, no one has appeared to put my great knowledge to use."

"Rubbish. That was my excuse to bring you down from Yorkshire."

She pretended to accept her long journey as a matter of business. Before she moved on from this place she would remind them all that business required payment.

"What business had you with me if it was not to aid your people with their carnival?"

He took her arm, led her unprotesting to see her face under the flaring torches. Trying to appear self-contained under his examination, she was rewarded by his dubious compliment. At least, she could enjoy the light in his eyes. "I'm glad you removed that ghastly bonnet and cloak."

As he studied her, she said, "Would you have looked twice at me if you hadn't seen the gypsy fortune-teller in Heaton Clough?"

"Probably not." He reached out to raise her chin. "Yes. I would have. There is something primitive about you. It's dazzling." He smiled. "And dangerous."

"Yes. I bite."

He laughed and withdrew his fingers. "Some day I won't let that disturb me."

"Not very flattering but I should have expected that, from the way you treat your betrothed."

She was surprised by his quiet, serious tone. "Elaine and I decided we were not meant for each other the day I sailed for Portugal. During the Spanish Campaign she became betrothed to a very pretty dandy, one of the Regent's cronies."

That might explain a good deal about Sir Anthony's attitude toward females.

119

He added, "When I returned after Waterloo, slightly the worse for wear, she reminded the world at one of Prinny's Brighton receptions that we were still betrothed but hadn't set the day. Being a gentleman, I said nothing, but I had a few thoughts on the subject."

"What will you do?"

"Who knows? What would you have me do?"

She said, "If you felt about marriage, especially to a Gentile, as I do, you would banish the idea, whether you were a gentleman or not."

"How true! And in my case, of course, I have a great passion for other-worldly creatures, primeval, you might say."

"In fact, rather like your ward's young admirer, Alexi. I daresay, if you knew him better, sir, you would appreciate his other-worldly character."

"I doubt it. He is—"

"A gypsy?"

He looked at her, frowning. "A thief and a coward. God knows what would become of Dilys, silly child, if he persuaded her to run away with him."

She discovered suddenly that they had walked into a gossiping, excited group of females whom Sir Anthony referred to as her admirers. Several crowded around her, asking questions about their own future and by the time she got them into place on the steps of the sheep wagon and looked back, Sir Anthony was waving to her from the outside of the crowd. The next minute he was in the midst of several tough-looking seamen very like French smugglers, this being a coast notorious for anything illegal.

She wondered that the Justice of the Peace of this area should be advising men who, in the normal course of events, were likely to be his prisoners. She suspected that if they had been gypsies they might very probably end in one of those carts bound for the Assizes, or somewhere just as unpleasant.

While she attended to the first of her patrons she found almost all of them wished their fortunes told not with the Tarot but with the crystal which gave out varied lights from the lanterns reflected in the wagon. The shillings piled up rapidly as the crystal lights mesmerised the women and helped them to imagine that they saw their answers in the glass.

Her imagination faded as the evening wore on. Either she was growing old at twenty-two or her mind was too much occupied with the incidents of the day, beginning and ending with Sir Anthony. A very annoying thought.

There were moments when the salty smell of the sea was vivid, though not unpleasant to her. It wasn't something she was used to, but it reminded her that the gypsy wanderers who had been her ancestors enjoyed almost all the unknown lands they encountered, in spite of the dangers and enmities they met or made by their peculiar lifestyle.

The audience gradually became younger, full of giggling, teasing girls and several youths, who, having paid their fee, asked ridiculous questions concerning other members of their group.

This provoked indignant, or sometimes laughing taunts, all of which Samara answered more or less from rote. Gradually, the questions that interested them most dealt with Samara herself.

Did she live in a sheep wagon?

Did she wear her gypsy costume all the time?

Did she move about the countryside all the time like the gypsies they had seen?

And finally, as they grew more daring:

Did gypsies really steal for a living?

It was a question she had been asked a hundred times and she said: "One must live. Just as you Gentiles must live. When necessary, we steal. But we do not harm you or cut your throats. Only your purses."

They were in excellent humour by now and almost everyone laughed. A couple of boys and a girl called out that they would like to live like that.

They were interrupted by Sir Anthony, who announced to the crowd, "Our gypsy lady will be back later. We need her to count the profits for the orphans."

A flattering number of the crowd grumbled and complained that they had more questions, but Samara came down off the steps to join Sir Anthony while several girls were still remarking on her costume.

As they went through the crowd, one of the girls reached for the big looped circle dangling from her left ear. Samara looked at her and the girl slowly withdrew her hand. Samara went on, smiling inwardly. She had learned early in life that there were methods more efficient than words or weapons to subdue inquisitive patrons.

Sir Anthony offered Samara his arm, but for a few seconds she was hardly aware of his presence. She had just seen a lean, bloodless-looking female turn from the crowd and start away. Samara was sure it must be the woman who had been staring at her early in the evening. Sir Anthony gave Samara a puzzled study, then felt she needed reassurance.

"You've been a great success. Are you tired?"

"Certainly not," she snapped and then, seeing his surprise at her manner, she gave him her best smile. "Perhaps a few nerves."

But it was there, the thought that the spying woman might be concerned with the Countess of Penryn and mean trouble.

Eleven

Half a dozen women were crowded into the wagon, all talking at once. Like so many female Gentiles, they seemed to be wearing the heavy odour of Attar of Roses or some other sweet perfume.

Curious, Samara thought, the difference in customs. They objected to the delicious odour of roasted meats, whose juices gypsy males rubbed on their arms. It was a small matter but it reminded her of who she was and how much longer than these Gentiles her own people had wandered the earth.

She came forward, made her way between the Countess and the lean, prying woman who now shrank away.

"Ah, our obliging friend." After the briefest look at Sir Anthony standing casually against the door with his arms folded, the Countess smiled charmingly at Samara. "I am told you were especially popular. Miss Reece will collect your contribution to our homeless children."

Miss Reece, as Samara found, was the lean woman who had apparently stood by during the last two hours, counting the patrons who visited the sheep wagon assigned to Samara.

Samara took the shillings and small coins out of her reticule, dropping them into Miss Reece's cupped hands. The woman counted them, dropping them into a delicate, black-lacquered box whose previous contents had been emptied into an over-sized reticule and the drawstrings tied.

The other women saw no problem and watched with interest, murmuring in satisfaction about the profits for the children's almshouse. But the Countess and Miss Reece were clearly puzzled. The Countess looked over the coins and an expression of surprise was shared by the two women. Miss Reece murmured, "I would swear I counted—"

Samara had been afraid there would be tricks afoot but the matter had gone exactly as she hoped it would. She stared at the Countess.

"Is there some reason why I may not add my few farthings to your charity, ladies? I myself am an orphan."

While the countess was thinking of a gracious answer the other women rectified the matter by thanking Samara several times. One of them even reminded them all that 'our guest' had contributed her talent and also several hours of her time to the orphans' charity.

All of this was received nicely, if cynically, by Samara, but to her surprise, Sir Anthony was even more cynical. He addressed no one in particular when he asked, "Will one of you ladies explain to me why Miss – er – Reece here seemed so disappointed that the young lady's contribution was even more then she expected?"

It was doubtful if anyone except the Countess and Miss Reece had expected that the gypsy entertainer would steal some of the contributions. But to Samara that did explain the curious disappointment of the two women when they discovered more, not less, contributed by someone the Countess clearly disliked.

Everyone spoke at once, exchanging puzzled looks and denying his suspicions.

Samara turned to leave the crowded wagon and was stopped for an instant by Sir Anthony's hand on her shoulder and his voice close behind her.

"I see my ward is waiting for us. She tells me you persuaded her the young gypsy is too immature for her. I want to thank you. She is in an excellent humour this past hour. That is rare these days."

Samara said honestly, "I can't imagine why she took seriously anything I told her." It was easier to say that than comment she could not quite believe Dilys Linden's sudden maturity.

"Well, whatever it is, I thank you. She has been in a high temper most of the time since we returned from the North."

Dilys waved to them, clearly including Samara in her greeting. She was looking flushed and prettier than ever when she curtsied to her guardian and Samara. Not many females of the girl's social position showed a gypsy such good manners. Perhaps it was the girl's way of showing Samara her gratitude for not having betrayed Alexi's presence. She wondered where the boy was now and tried not to make the movement obvious when she glanced over the still-noisy, moving crowd on the strand of the beach.

She was relieved that no one in the immediate crowd resembled Alexi. Like Samara herself his natural complexion and colouring were far darker than anyone she could see as she went down the steps and found herself surrounded in the flaring lights by both Dilys and her guardian.

"Well, ask her," Sir Anthony said impatiently.

Dilys giggled, puzzling Samara by her pleasure over something that would make not only her guardian but Samara happy.

"She will love it," Dilys went on. "Won't she, cousin? It would be so unusual."

Sir Anthony said, "Never mind that. Ask her."

Samara doubted very much if this surprise would please her. She prepared herself for cool gratitude and a refusal of whatever they had in mind.

"We want you to spend a few nights at our home in Rye before you return to Yorkshire. You can almost see our hilltop from here."

To Samara it was worse than she had expected. She had never slept in an 'elegant' house, like one obviously belonging to a Justice of the Peace, a magistrate used to sentencing gypsies to prison or the gallows, or transportation.

It was not entirely that she feared she would humiliate herself by her ignorance of almost everything in such a house. Even if these people pretended not to notice her alien presence, the servants would know at once. And above all, she would not be free.

She would have to conduct herself with great care. Even her travel clothing would be despised, and her forthright manner would never be appropriate in Anthony Linden's house. Or worse, among his friends.

"That is very kind of you, and of Sir Anthony. But I am on my way to Dorset to visit my people." Marika and Stefan would be surprised to see her this early in the season. Generally, they took her up in their wagons when they came through in late spring. "Besides," she added, "Sir Anthony is not fond of gypsies."

"Some. Not all. In any case, you are coming with us. I sent for the carriage. Dilys likes to ride in great style."

"I came down here in it, looking splendid," Dilys assured her. "If I can't have that gypsy friend of yours, Samara, I may as well content myself with Elaine Penryn's nephew, Gareth, and he will see me drive away before his eyes if he is still here. He always envies that carriage. Now, wasn't that a delicious surprise, Samara?"

"Delightful, Miss Linden. But my family in Dorset will be expecting me."

Sir Anthony picked up Samara's portmanteau and bundle of costumes, then hesitated, looking at Samara as if genuinely disappointed.

"Would you object to one night, or perhaps two? I can escort you personally to Dorset." He had signalled an elderly man in livery to whom Dilys was now talking, and before Samara could think of a sufficiently strong excuse Sir Anthony gave her a smile that she found surprisingly winning. It was not the air of command that she associated with the magistrate

129

responsible for the unfortunates she had seen in the carts on the High Road.

"Surely your people will not leave Dorset without you? And only one . . . or two nights." He added suddenly in the teasing tone he had used with her once or twice, "I promise your bedchamber door may be bolted from the inside."

It was an awkward situation. She had far too much pride to tell him she had never stayed in a mansion before. Even worse, she dreaded finding herself the object of secret jeers, amusement and gossip that was sure to spread among Sir Anthony's associates.

But he offered his hand now, closing it over hers, and while she was still repeating, "It is impossible," he reminded her, "You can do nothing at the moment. In an hour or two it will be midnight. You must have decent accommodations tonight. There are no inns of any consequence. We can talk of your future plans tomorrow."

She had expected one of Sir Anthony's servants to drive her to a local inn. If the landlord refused to take her – and her people were often refused – she would pay to sleep in a loft over a stable, which would be reasonably comfortable.

She started to tell him so but Dilys began to look uneasy. What was in the girl's conniving little brain? It had nothing to do with the Countess of Penryn's nephew. No matter what the girl protested, she couldn't have forgotten Alexi that quickly. Not even a sudden quarrel between them would have produced her odd tension and her furtive glances at

Samara when the gypsy was in conversation with Sir Anthony.

While Sir Anthony was explaining the discomfort and problems she would face if she left tonight, the old coachman approached Dilys and murmured something. The girl called to her guardian.

"He says the team is growing restless."

Sir Anthony looked at Samara who shrugged, giving in reluctantly. She knew she could leave the Linden household secretly if she chose to go.

Then, too, she was not at all sure what she intended to do when she left the magistrate. She wanted to travel, to wander and see the world of her ancestors before returning home, wherever that should prove to be.

She and Dilys were bundled into the old but well-kept landau and Dilys surprisingly announced her preference for riding with her back to the coachman, leaving to Sir Anthony the seat beside their guest.

Her guardian's eyebrows raised at such unaccustomed generosity but he got in with a knowing smile at Samara.

As the horses made their way along the narrow road away from the beach where the noise and smoking lights continued, Sir Anthony remarked to Dilys, "Let us hope Elaine's nephew saw your handsome departure, though I never thought he would be impressed by our ancient equipage."

Samara wondered if he suspected, as she did, that the girl's talk about Gareth Penryn was a lie. But she said nothing and noted that Dilys laughed away his remark.

It was less than half an hour before Sir Anthony looked out as the coachman pulled up his team.

"I trust you aren't too tired. We walk up the hill."

Samara was amused. "I spend my life walking, sir."

They left the coachman, his carriage and team at the stables and started up one of the cobbled streets, past numerous Tudor dwellings and shops, lit only by the stars. Dilys groaned at the rough cobbles but Samara had been seated for hours and enjoyed the long strides.

When they were near the top of the hill she was startled to see a little graveyard with large, standing gravestones, which seemed to be the centre of the village. Facing the graveyard was a half-timbered two-storey house which was large but surprisingly modest for the home of the local Justice of the Peace.

Sir Anthony pointed at the view below the house on the Channel side. She looked almost directly down and saw the long strand of beach where several longboats and a dory were pulled up but seemed untended.

Probably, Samara thought, the lugger out beyond the breakers had been unloaded and was sailing away while local seamen were somewhere in Rye making a contraband delivery.

The area was briefly interesting to Samara, but she thought it strange that Sir Anthony didn't find it sombre and depressing as a home, after his years on the Continent, and a life of danger, colour and adventure.

A female servant with a branched candlestick opened the door to them and led them through a stone passageway and up a heavy, dark staircase to the chambers abovestairs.

The big clock on the landing struck midnight and Dilys looked at it as though it might be lying.

"Heavens! Half the night is gone. Poor Samara. She must be dreadfully tired after her travels today and all those tiresome women tonight."

"I'm sure she is tired of your chattering," her guardian told her.

Dilys started down the corridor which was colder than the sheep wagon where Samara had read the crystal earlier in the evening. Samara called after her, "Thank you, Miss Linden. You've been very kind."

Dilys waved without looking around. She disappeared into a room at the far end of the corridor.

Meanwhile, Sir Anthony introduced his housekeeper, Mrs Powell, to her and the woman looked over Samara's gypsy bright costume, her very noticeable earrings, responding to the introduction with a brief, "Ay, ma 'am." She then addressed Sir Anthony. "Will the – the lady desire anything more tonight?"

Sir Anthony did not seem to mind her curtness. His manner was equally curt.

"Miss Samara will give you her orders."

"Nothing," Samara said briskly, only just refraining from one of what had been called her 'horrendous' looks.

The housekeeper curtsied to her employer and added to him, "There is mulled wine on the nightstand and cakes if Miss is hungry in the night."

In spite of this polite touch, Samara was relieved to

see her go and then, catching Sir Anthony's eye, she smiled. "No. She doesn't frighten me."

He had opened the door and waited as she psased him. He said, "No. But you frighten her."

That did make her laugh.

He lowered his head suddenly and kissed her cheek, then drew back, but the grin remained.

"What? Are your teeth less sharp tonight?"

"Try the bolt on this door and you will find out."

He pinched her chin and the next minute he was gone, with the door closed behind him.

She thought, I know better than to let myself become attached even briefly to a Gentile, and worse of all, a Justice of the Peace. Absurd!

It must stop here. She hated what his position in life meant to her people. She did not like his dreadful house, his servants who would despise her and have the Gentiles' idea that she was no better than a vagabond. She and Sir Anthony had nothing whatever in common and never would have.

Her fingertips touched her cheek. The magistrate's lips had barely grazed her flesh, yet she still felt the heated touch. She dared not go further with him. Eventually, it could lead to nothing. Merely his brief *affaire* with a common female vagabond, as his own courtroom would call her. She thought better of herself than that.

How many gypsy women had he condemned in his legal capacity, perhaps when he was done with them?

But not this gypsy!

Twelve

S amara removed her cloak and looked around the bedroom. The furnishings were heavy and more than plentiful. They made the room seem stifling, added to the smouldering fire in the grate which took up half of one wall. There was a huge wardrobe next to the door and under the window a shaving stand with a small mirror.

But the bed was the worst. Enormous, with a little flight of steps needed, even by a tall woman like Samara, to reach what must be three mattresses. The bed was curtained in velvet, crimson, of course, so that the horrid thing appeared even more stifling. The floor was covered by a threadbare carpet from the Near East on which stood a portable bath whose water was still warm. A piece of highly perfumed soap was melting in the water.

It was the only item in the room that was useful. Samara went to the door, shot the bolt and came back to remove her clothing. She appreciated the thoughtfulness of the bath after three days of travel. Since she usually wore sandals over her bare feet, she felt the constant need of a foot bath, though she was well aware that someone in the house believed gypsies were even worse than Gentiles. Neither gypsies nor Gentiles bathed on more occasions than were strictly necessary.

She screwed up her hair, pinning it with a black hair bodkin, stripped off her skirts, blouse and chemise and stepped into the bath. It was necessary to tuck her long legs up against her breasts but this proved easy enough for her agile and energetic body. The water was barely warm, but it wasn't the first time this had happened and she scrubbed enthusiastically, rubbing with the towels.

The mulled wine afterward and the very sweet sweetcakes, the way she liked them, were welcome. She put on a clean petticoat, as usual, unlocked the door again and climbed up into bed. It was obviously made for a lady of dainty habits. The minute she sank down on the mattresses she felt as if she were drowning. Everything sank like clouds beneath her. No one could possibly prefer such a bed. She doubted very much if Sir Anthony slept in this fashion. If so, he must have found Portugal and Spain remarkably changed since Samara's gypsy ancestors lived as wanderers over the Iberian Peninsula.

She got up, sat on the bed for a moment, sinking all the time, and finally made a decision, throwing the thick blankets, sheets and coverlet off in a heap on the floor.

A few minutes later, having wrapped her body in a blanket, with another blanket on the floor beneath her, and a wadded-up petticoat beneath her head, she lay down, covered herself and was about to go to sleep in comfort when someone rapped on the door.

She asked who it was and then sat straight up, hearing Sir Anthony's voice.

A Splash of Rubies

"Are you warm enough? It will be fairly cold before morning."

As she was about to refuse whatever he had in mind, he opened the door and strolled in loaded with blankets. He looked around the room in the flickering light from the hall candles.

"I haven't invited you in," she reminded him, pretending not to be in the least embarrassed.

But it was his turn to be shocked. "What the devil are you doing on the floor?"

"If I were permitted without interruption, I would be asleep."

He came into the room, still dressed in tan pantaloons and reasonably unwrinkled white linen shirt but minus the elegant coat and white stock he had worn earlier in the evening.

"I came to see how you are doing, if there was anything you wished. It's damned dark in here!" He took a few steps back, reached for a simple candleholder off the nearby credenza and lighted his way back into the room.

He held the candlestick over her while she protested that it was dripping wax on her petticoat. He grinned at that and studied her as she sat there, most of her bosom exposed to his view. She wanted to cover herself but that would only give him satisfaction in the thought that he had embarrassed her.

"Enchanting," he remarked, though her lower limbs were still covered by the blanket. "I was sure you would be."

"Thank you. Goodnight."

137

He leaned down and with his free hand, raised her chin. "I merely wanted to ask if there was anything you needed, you witch."

The smooth brass-gold of her flesh swelled under the muslin of her petticoat. She became aware that she had exposed her breasts to his interested gaze and she kicked at his ankles. She snapped, "Remember, I can still bite."

For a moment his hand lingered over her throat as she stiffened, aware of the excitement of his touch. Then he stood, held the candle aloft and in quite a different mood, enquired in a businesslike way, "May I ask a perfectly proper question?"

"If you must." She was covering herself and tried to be just as businesslike as he was.

"Why are you sleeping on the cold floor?"

Pulling herself together, she said airily, "I have slept out in the moors on harder ground than your floor."

"Amazing. I have done that, but it was all business. War business. Let me show you how comfortable a bed can be."

She had tangled her legs between the blanket and her petticoat and he set the candle on the bedside stand, then reached for her. She drew back but realised as she found herself lifted into his arms that he was stronger than others whose ambition to conquer her had left them somewhat the worse for their efforts. It was the memory of those others and the ignominious failure to arouse her own emotions that made her put so much violence into her struggle. But the painful grip of his arms proved more than a match for her.

138

"There. Admit this bed is more comfortable."

He dropped her on the bed, despite her flailing legs and bruised arms. He looked down into her eyes as she gritted her teeth and determined to bite him.

He put his hands out to keep her from falling off the high bed and she was more gently imprisoned beneath his arms and his body. For a few seconds he stared into her eyes, then bent his head and covered her mouth with his own lips.

There was an unexpected tenderness in his kiss. It left her breathless, unable to cry out, but it aroused her in a totally new way. As if he had drawn all the strength from her body, she found herself surrendering to the violent beating of her heart, and felt her arms freed. She raised them around his neck and her body seemed drained of power to release herself.

She knew he was stripping her body of the wrinkled petticoat and his fingers, surprisingly sensuous, began to move over her flesh, his lips following their touch. With a desire she did not recognise she drew him to her bared loins and yielded to the heat of desire within her . . .

It was only afterward that she realised the emotion she felt was new to her. Something her entire life had waited for. She had never before experienced the wild burst of pure joy that she knew during those moments of their love-making.

It was all over too soon, because it had to be over.

She recovered herself.

Everything, every act and event in her life, told her she could not depend upon the passion she had felt tonight for this Gentile.

As she freed herself from his body and his arms, he was a little breathless and she was glad. At least, he would not think he was easily aroused without touching his emotions in any way. What of tomorrow? And the days and nights to follow? She knew better than to find herself dependent on him, whatever the excitement she felt in his arms.

He controlled the feelings he had betrayed and was looking very much easier, almost amused, as she made her bed on the floor again.

He got up, watching her arrange the extra petticoat as a pillow once more and pull up the wrinkled blankets.

"I knew I wanted you those first minutes at the gypsy horse fair," he said in an almost emotionless voice. "More than that. And you want me too. Admit it, Samara."

She assured him, "You are one of the most attractive *goys* I have ever known."

This seemed to set his teeth on edge. He asked, "How many *goys* have you known . . . in this way?"

She was about to ignore this but blurted out, "There was no feeling. Only brutality. I felt nothing. I hated him. I was thirteen."

"Good God!" He reached down and covered her chilled fingers with his own. "I had no notion. Do you really hate me so much?"

She was thoughtful. "No. For a minute – two or three minutes – I did forget. And it was different."

His hand went to her face. "I'm glad it was different. I want our relationship to be different. More like—"

He hesitated. "Like your own father and mother. Genuine."

She laughed hoarsely. "Oh, yes. Like that. My father was a Gentile. He grew tired of my mother after I was born. I was three or four before I heard him call her 'a dirty gypsy'. They quarrelled all the time. In the tinker's wagon one day they overturned. She died that night."

He shook his head. His hand, still warm, moved to her face and hair as she looked up.

"And your father?"

She shrugged. "He died a year or so later in a drunken fight and his mother, my grandmother, came from Heaton Clough to fetch me."

As if he were trying to take her mind off these painful memories, he said, "So that's why I met you in Yorkshire. But you have very little dialect."

She explained, "Grandmother was a governess for many years."

Disregarding this detail, he looked at her for a long moment. She stared up at him, defiant.

He asked finally, "Do you forgive me?"

"Did you mean it?"

That made him angry. "Of course, I did."

She smiled a little. "I believe you love me now. There is pity too. But it will pass."

"Can't you love me a little? Give me a chance to prove I mean it?"

"I might. If you were someone else." She raised both hands to his and he took them in his palms. "Or if you needed me. But you don't. You have everything. Our being together can only bring you disgrace."

141

He squeezed her hands painfully between his. "Listen to me. I came back from the war feeling nothing. I had no love, no cares. I tried at first to spend time making a young lady of Dilys. She was as bored as I was. Elaine – but you guessed her indifference at once. And then, there you were."

"A dirty gypsy."

"No, damn you! An exotic creature not quite human. I wanted to tame this glorious bird. Not any more. I think I would prefer your life. As you are."

What nonsense he talked! Dear nonsense, if she could believe it as he obviously did, for the moment.

"You'll feel different in the morning, sir."

He let her hands go and said, "Promise to think over what I've told you?"

"I will."

Always. She would never forget what this fascinating, dynamic Gentile had told her, and he believed it. She felt sure of that. Whatever he might think in weeks and months to come.

"Goodnight. And forgive me?"

He leaned over and kissed her cheek. She teased, "I won't bite you."

Then he went out into the hall, closing the door gently behind him.

She ran her hands over her body, beneath the petticoat. It seemed as though his love-making had cleansed her of other memories. If only Sir Anthony Linden had been one of her own people!

Thirteen

S amara had a troubled sleep. She could not stop
thinking of the one man whom she knew she could
have loved. Then she began to be more aware of his
world, the smell of the sea which still seemed strange,
rough, but not unpleasant. Just before dawn she heard
shouting, grumbling and some off-key singing on a
path that arose from the long strand of beach far
below.

She untangled herself from her improvised bedding
and went to the window. The crowd, mostly young
adults, was climbing up the cliffside. They all seemed
to have enjoyed the 'gypsy carnival' though some were
dressed as cavaliers, saucy milkmaids and an occasional Barbary pirate. Would Sir Anthony have them
all manacled and jailed if he heard them?

So this was the civilised world, enjoying itself, pretending to live a gypsy's life! No one was ever happy
being what he was. Small wonder that they missed the
essential life of the wanderers they imitated.

She turned back into the room, reflecting that she
herself had been happy wandering the moors of Yorkshire's West Riding. More and more she had discov-

ered that if she was tired of her grandmother's 'coteen' and the eternal strangers among whom she lived, she was no happier than Gentiles. Their imitation happiness, with no real freedom, was not what she wanted in her life, Painful as it was, she had been right not to listen to Anthony Linden.

Somehow, she would forget him and go adventuring after she left this place. And soon, before her passion for him took over her commonsense and her own will.

Where would she go? Not back to where her parents had met in Ireland. Not even the Dorset heath where her gypsy band made their home, but out to wander the world, see a thousand new things.

While she was considering how her last Tarot reading would fit into her new plans, or even warn her against them, she fell asleep, dreaming of the Justice of the Peace.

She was awakened by the sunlight and the realisation that she must take care of the floor full of bedclothes before the housekeeper saw them, and then she must wash and dress before anyone else saw her. She was brushing her hair after dressing when a rapping on the door startled her. She opened the door, expecting the housekeeper, and found Dilys Linden, young, nervous, looking back over her shoulder into the hall.

Surprised by the sight of the girl, Samara asked, "Is something wrong?"

"Oh, yes. Yes!" Dilys whispered in an agitated way. "May I come in? It's confidential."

Samara had little interest in the girl's problems,

especially if they were secretive. "You had best speak to your guardian, miss."

More whispering and furtives glances around the hall.

"I can't. He was called out half an hour ago. About a seaman who struck and killed his wife."

Delightful people, she thought, but opened the door for the girl and then closed it when Dilys had rustled in and asked her, "Bolt it, please."

With the door bolted Dilys looked around, puzzled a moment over the bedclothes on the bed, and then surprised Samara by asking, "Didn't you bring your Tarot cards?"

"Certainly." Samara reached into her bundle of costumes and brought out the small, polished ivory box. The key was strung around her neck and without removing it, she unlocked the box, careful to do so under the girl's eyes. The cards were worn and Dilys touched them gingerly. "They are dark and dirty. They must have been in the box for years."

"They belonged to my mother. She left them to me. Why? Do you want a reading?"

Dilys looked ashamed of her request. "I'm sorry. But I do want to know what to do. You see, I can't resist dear Alexi. He tells me to do something, and I obey. Tell me what will happen if – if I do obey Alexi."

Whatever Samara's doubts about Dilys Linden, she never lost her own belief in the future as shown by the Tarot cards. It was too close to her childhood and every day in her life since then.

She took the pack to the nightstand and cut the

145

cards several times, watching Dilys. As she had suspected, these motions meant nothing to her. She even seemed impatient.

"Never mind that. I must know soon."

"What is your question to be?" Samara asked, realising the girl had no interest in a reading. What else did she want?

Dilys explained belatedly, "I just want to discover if I may be happy with him."

"You would marry someone so different from your own people?"

Samara thought: even I know better than to plan such a disastrous life.

Dilys shrugged. "Well, I must marry someone, to be free of Cousin Anthony and to get my jewels." She looked up at Samara with pitiful innocence. "I told Alexi where my cousin hid my rubies. And now, perhaps . . . Perhaps I was too hasty. But you see, I can't prevent him from knowing now, even if I wanted to. Of course, I could try," she ventured, with a side long look at Samara.

"But you don't wish to," Samara remarked coldly.

"Well, you see, I'm not strong like you." She looked out the window at the morning sunlight and returned her attention to Samara's long fingers as they set down the cards. "I am so desperate for time. Can this be settled quickly?"

"Certainly. Cut the cards as you choose and take your first card from the pack. This refers to your past." She found this almost laughable at the girl's age, but Dilys, moving rapidly and clumsily, reached for the deck.

Two cards flew out of the pack and onto the carpet. Dilys reached for them and began to turn one card around. Interested always in such signs, Samara stopped her.

Dilys hesitated. "But this one is the wrong way up."

"That may be part of your past. There is no discipline in the Emperor Negative."

"An old man in my life? How horrid! I suppose it is my cousin Anthony."

Samara's brows raised. "An old man? Your Cousin Anthony?"

"Well," Dilys reminded her, "he must be thirty if he is a day."

Samara could not deny that. He was probably a little over thirty, but she found Dilys more and more juvenile. She asked, "What is the other card that fell?"

Dilys looked down, picked up the second card and set it on the nightstand beside the first card. "At least, it is straight up. It is getting late and I haven't had my breakfast. Let me take another card."

Samara let her make the choice, explaining, "But it will be your third card. Your future."

"Yes, yes. I know." Dilys drew the card and groaned. "Another upside down." Then her eyes widened at the two figures whose exposed sexual organs fascinated her. She gave one of her giggles. "I know. I will have a wonderful life, full of romance."

Samara looked at the card, then at Dilys. The girl was waiting so she said merely, "It is The Lovers, but negative. If you choose wrongly, you will end in disaster."

Dilys thrust her hand out and knocked the Tarot deck onto the floor. "You are making this up because you hate me, because of what happened in Yorkshire."

Samara began to pick up the cards. She was contemptuous but suspicious too.

"Is Alexi hereabouts? Does he really know where your guardian's jewellery is?"

"Of course. I told you. He made me tell him." Dilys broke off abruptly. "Do you take me for a fool?"

Samara could not resist saying with heavy irony, "How well you know Alexi!"

But she did not believe it. Alexi was charming and flirtatious and certainly fond of anything he could obtain without labour or danger. That was the limit of his talents. He was neither brave nor clever enough to rob Sir Anthony, although he would certainly accept the profits from a robbery.

Dilys seemed not to have given the message of the cards much attention. She started out the door with a careless air as if her errand was done.

Samara stood there watching her. The girl stopped in the hall, smiled mischievously and gave her a charming little wink.

"I could tell you where my cousin locks up the jewellery that I am supposed to wear on special occasions. Would you like to know?"

"No, Miss Linden. I would not."

Impudent little witch!

She decided to suggest that Sir Anthony should at least conceal the jewellery more safely.

Dilys pouted and went onto the staircase and did not look back.

Samara checked to be sure the coins in the little pockets of her petticoat were safe, took a heavy shawl out of her portmeanteau, and went out into the hall. She met a buxom young girl bringing a pitcher of warm water to her room and Samara asked if Sir Anthony had returned. The girl looked at her with some interest but assured her, "He's always busy after there's a dreadful murderer is took off to wait trial. It'll be the rope for sure. Nasty wife-killer!"

"Yes. Where would I find the Justice?"

"In the tavern, miss, most like. He went off with no breakfast." She added, "You'll find the tavern past the graveyard, down the hill a few steps."

Samara thanked her and went down the stairs. A male servant was busy polishing bric-a-brac in a salon on the lower floor. From the glance Samara caught of the salon it was more like a comfortable sitting room and she was impressed by this mark of simplicity. It was hard to believe these simple tastes belonged to the magistrate of this area so near to London and with constant dealings with France. She thought better of Sir Anthony. It certainly was a far cry from his greedy luxury-loving little ward.

Very few people were out on the cobbled streets, possibly because the graveyard seemed so close, or merely because the enjoyment the previous night had left the village exhausted. Samara looked around. Those few on the street stared back. She looked her most forbidding. Even though the peasant-style green shawl had fallen from the crown of her head to her shoulders, there was, as Dr Halperin had once said timidly, a look about her that did not welcome the acquaintance of casual strangers. Though she knew this, she was quite happy that it was so.

Two boys rolling hoops along the street collided near Samara, barely missing her. She looked over at them. Her toe in its sandal scooted the lost hoop toward the boys and the one who had fallen yelled to his friend, "Come back! Help me up. It's one of them dirty gypsies." Another yell pierced the air and he fell back on the cobblestones. He was still scrambling to get to his feet as the second boy yelled to him.

"Come along a' me. We're late."

Samara took a step toward the fallen boy. She reached out, wondering why she troubled to give him a hand up but he drew back, avoiding her touch, and she stood over him with her hands on her hips.

The noise had finally aroused the men in the tavern and the tapster came out to wave off the boys with his apron.

"Be quiet, will 'e now? We've the magistrate inside with a meetin' and there'll be no nonsense."

Hearing this, Samara took a few steps away, intending to wait somewhere until Sir Anthony's business, or his breakfast, might be finished. But the boys had been heard inside and they scuttled away. Samara looked back to see what had sent them on their way.

It was the sight of the Justice of the Peace himself

who came out, grinned at the sight of the running boys trying to roll their hoops as they ran.

Sir Anthony saw Samara and came over to her.

"Frightening the infants now, I see."

He took her hand away from her hip in an excellent humour. For an instant she thought he would raise it to his lips like a gallant at the Prince Regent's court and she would have laughed at the absurdity. Instead, he taunted her while her fingers were imprisoned, "May I hope you've come enticing me to breakfast with you? I have been too busy to eat a bite while the arguments proceeded. I promise not to be afraid of you like your young friends."

She forced a cool, businesslike manner. "Not my friends, sir. I do have a matter to bring to your attention, though. When you are not so busy."

"Good. Let us say now." He tucked her hand against his close-fitting jacket. "Have you breakfasted yet?"

"Yes," she lied. "I must talk to you."

"Nothing easier. I am giving myself a moment's respite and will walk you back to the house."

They had only walked a few steps when he prompted her: "Well, has the emperor escaped from St Helena? Is our noble Prince Regent taking over from his Papa? Or – on the more charming side – are you going to think over last night and let me prove I am sincere?"

She said abruptly, "I suggest you conceal your jewellery from—"

"From you?" He was smiling.

"And from everyone else."

"I know. You don't trust my saintly ex-betrothed."

"I am not talking of the Countess, but of Miss Linden."

He still smiled, but there was an edge to his remark. "You haven't mentioned the rogue in Yorkshire. Your friend Alexi Something – I know you have a fondness for the fellow."

She stared at him, caught unaware by this absurd suspicion. "You might have said my son. I've known Alexi since he was born. But in any case, I believe you should change the hiding place today. At once."

She could scarcely believe his dislike of Alexi was concerned more with her than with his ward. The boy was little more than a child, mentally, in any case.

"Alexi's parents, Marika and Stefan, are the only relations I care for in the world. We are of the same band."

He was silent briefly but seemed satisfied. "I'm glad. I suddenly had a notion the little bastard was lurking about here and he is certainly capable of stealing my mother's jewels."

"Then the rubies do not belong to Dilys? She told me they were her inheritance and you were holding them from her."

He shrugged. "Dilys was completely spoiled by her mother, who reared her. She died while I was in Spain and left the girl in my charge. Thanks to a nasty little sabre slice in Belgium I didn't find out any of this until late last year."

"Meanwhile, sir, I must be ready in time for the London mail," she reminded him. "Once there I will be on my way to Dorset."

She had shaken him. "You can't mean that," he said abruptly. "We will dispose of that later. I'll escort you to the house before I return to that wrangling in the tavern."

They walked back up to Linden House and were facing the graveyard when she asked, "Don't you find the view from your home depressing?"

He looked over at the centre of the square carelessly.

"I was born here. My people lived here in the sixteenth century when Queen Elizabeth dubbed it Royal Rye. I'm told they were very proud of this little home of pirates, smugglers and other unsavoury people."

She laughed and was pleased when he said, "I like your laugh. Deep and strong. It's not a silly female's laugh. But then, you aren't a silly female, are you?"

She thought: probably a compliment. At all events I will accept it as one, and long after I've gone from here, I will think of his voice when he said it.

Remembering what she must do, now that she had warned him about the jewels, she said, "I have things that must be done, sir, and I know you have too. Excuse me."

He looked concerned, called, "Not yet. We haven't discussed—"

"Later," she promised, knowing it was a promise she would not keep.

She went up to her room, passing the housekeeper without addressing her. The woman looked after her with one eyebrow raised.

Samara went to the bedchamber assigned to her and

noticed that her portmanteau stood by the door and the bundle of her costumes was carefully obvious in the middle of the floor.

She collected her property, changed her shawl for her cloak and went toward the stairs with her luggage. She heard footsteps coming up and hurried to the front of the hall. She was alone there and went down rapidly. She stooped once to look back on the lower floor below the staircase but luckily there were only sounds of broomstraws sticking at the salon walls as a servant girl worked in the small salon.

Instead of taking the main cobbled street past the tavern she walked to the narrow and less popular street on the side of the hill and strode down toward the high road to wait for the London mail coach.

In some ways she was glad to have the relationship with Sir Anthony done for ever. It had been impossible from the beginning. The difference between the magistrate and herself had never been sharper.

She remembered vividly the sight of those carts with their wretched human cargo bound for a fate she didn't want to think about. It was better to find once more the people like Marika and Stefan who had accepted her among their own kind.

At the foot of the hill she looked back, said a mental goodbye to the exciting but unattainable Anthony Linden. His life was certainly not hers. She hurried on.

Would he succeed in settling matters with his ward? She hoped he would take the girl out of Alexi's reach, not for the girl's sake, or for Alexi's but to save Marika the deep pain of the stupid boy's loss.

Nevertheless, every time she heard the wind rustle in the bushes on the side of the road, she turned, wondering if Sir Anthony might, by accident, be riding along this road. Or perhaps not by accident . . .

On one of these dreamy thoughts, she heard the very sound she had thought to hear. Hoofbeats of several riders, and something else, the rattle of wheels on a cart.

A cart in which they carried prisoners to the Assizes. Or worse. To the Old Bailey. She started to run.

Fourteen

S he was fast on her feet but even Samara could hardly out-run the horsemen on their mounts, and a cart pulled by a powerful dray-horse.

Fortunately, the roadside was lined on the easterly side by bushes, shrubs and an occasional sand-hill. She found the dry and prickly bushes better protection and made her way behind them. The riders galloped past, followed by the rattling cart.

She stopped to take breath, relieved to see herself alone again with only the faint stirring of the breeze for company in the rushes further toward the Channel.

The mail coach would be along soon and take her aboard. Much depended on how late the driver was and very possibly what extra shillings she would pay him over the rate.

She waited a few minutes, while several horses and riders passed her on their way to Rye and the south, interspersed by an old carriage drawn by an equally unenthusiastic four-horse team. Then she made her way rapidly along the high road.

The brush at the side of the road spread out and finally disappeared. There was no further cover. She increased her pace and suddenly heard the heavy beat of horses from the northerly direction taken by the local riding officers who had passed her without knowing it.

She would not likely be their business unless Sir Anthony used them, as she first had feared. But surely her departure would not concern the local Riding Officers. Their business was with smuggling.

She thought of crossing the road where a clump of trees might provide shelter when the horsemen appeared just as she started across. There was nothing for it but to brave it out. She stopped to avoid being struck by the leading mount and waited patiently. With her portmanteau and bundle of clothes she resembled a woman of the lower classes, which in many respects, she was. If she and her people were of any class. They would probably take more notice of her if they decided she was a gypsy. These days the members of any band seldom travelled alone.

The two leading horsemen pulled up and one of them trotted his mount around her.

"You, there! Where are you bound?"

"The London coach . . . sir."

"And no doubt, you've come from Rye?"

There were no laws against that, surely!

"Ay, sir. The carnival for the Orphans Charity last night."

The rugged officer with him nodded. "They called it gypsy. Just funning, you know."

The first who was younger and apparently anxious

to assert himself, said sharply, "Then she knows where to find 'em. Speak up, you. Where'll we find 'em?"

"Find who?" She almost writhed when she had to answer him so politely.

The young officer ordered her, "Raise your head!" He looked at his companion. "A gypsy, or I'm a Dutchman. Mind those eyes? She's the one, right enough. She'll know."

She said, "I haven't seen any of the band for weeks, sir."

"Likely! She knows. She's his partner."

The older man considered her. "Could be another gypsy hereabouts."

"That's like you, Sam'l. Show you a pretty face and you'll call her innocent every time. This one's a part of it, I tell you. Let her go and she'll have your purse and that clicker of yours afore you can swing a cat."

Sam'l agreed without saying so and signalled one of the other officers with the cart and horse behind them.

The officer dismounted, jerked her portmanteau out of her hand and threw it into the cart behind him. He was about to pull the bundle of her precious costumes out of her other hand when she kicked him across the lower thigh and slammed the bundle against his arm.

Sam'l laughed but stopped suddenly when the officer who had been attacked swore and shot his hand across Samara's cheek. She had braced herself and did not let this painful blow knock her down. She started to reach under her coat to the little knife in her sash but knew that was a sure way to the gallows. She stared hard at him without blinking and the friendlier Sam'l called out to his colleague angrily, "Here now. None a' that. Lift her into the cart. And gently, man! We'll see what she knows later."

The officer who had exchanged blows with her hesitated and the fourth officer beside the cart, a burly fellow formerly silent, pointed out, "We'd ought to tie the hellcat's wrists."

The young officer motioned to him and as Samara pulled her hands away the officer seized her wrists and bound them together with a stout cord while she winced but made no sound. With her eyes blazing she managed a taunting smile. He set her on her feet in the cart.

The horses all started off. Rubbing her wrists against the wooden side of the cart to resore circulation, she looked out on the road ahead. The little group was off again toward Rye. If they were returning to Rye, she would probably appear before Sir Anthony Linden. Was this some sort of joke to keep her from going off to Dorset? Or did she flatter herself?

For a woman with her feelings about nature versus confinement, there could be only the horrors of prison ahead of her. The only thing she could think of that would condemn her must be concerned with Alexi. The officers' reference to gypsies made her suspect the worst.

The sun and the wind off the Channel made the flesh of her cheek burn where it had been struck, and the cheekbone itself ached but the numbness of her wrists was harder to bear. No matter. There were worse things in the world. Anything would be better than perpetual confinement and she had always been reasonably confident in her open and outdoor world.

She told herself that Sir Anthony found her at least temporarily interesting, perhaps even a romantic figure, as he had definitely indicated. She would never give such freedom for her emotions. The gulf was too wide, and even though he fascinated her as no other man had, nothing about his life, except himself, was anything but a gloomy death in life to her.

By the time the Riding Officers reached Rye shortly after noon with their prisoner, the town was up and about, having survived the charity carnival and returned to their usual busy work day.

The Riding Officers received a good many stares as they dismounted and reached up into the cart to life out Samara.

Curiously enough, the officer who had struck her after she kicked him helped her out of the cart. She was amused at the gesture, almost as though she were the Prince Regent's daughter. At least, it impressed several passers-by when the group of officers walked up over the cobbles toward Sir Anthony's house at the crest of the hill with Samara in their midst and one of them carrying her luggage. Had they decided she was someone personally known to the magistrate? She breathed easier. This might be in her favour, depending on Sir Anthony's whim.

With Samara between the first two Riding Officers and the others following they came rapidly to the Linden house. Samara paid little attention to the people around her, but she wondered where Sir Anthony might be.

The young officer gave the brass knocker an authoritative clang. The door was opened by the housekeeper whose reception of her last night she remembered very well. Seeing the officers with Samara today, she gave her a thin smile and stood aside for them all to enter.

The officers appeared used to discussing cases in the magistrate's house, but Sir Anthony was nowhere to be seen. The house was surprisingly silent, considering how talkative and self-assertive Dilys Linden usually was.

Meanwhile, the young officer asked if Sir Anthony would be returning soon.

The housekeeper was not in the least afraid of these officials.

"Sir Anthony has been on the sands, interviewing the dock workers and whatever ships are laying off-shore here. There is a possibility some may have sailed in the last hour on short hauls to Hastings or other ports."

The men looked at each other and the young officer in charge said, "We had best wait. We have taken a partner in the affair."

"Her being a gypsy too," put in one of the other officers. "Sir Anthony – he'll have his proof right enough."

So that was it! Sir Anthony, for all his flirting with her, had sent them after her.

Gentiles! You could never trust their word. Rubbing

her wrists, she stood by the long window of the salon, looking down toward the beach and the distant Channel, with the reflection that she had been right about the Gentiles during most of her life. Her Christian grandmother would have behaved much as Sir Anthony did now. Because his stupid, spoiled ward, Dilys, had done something or other, probably run away, it must be the fault of Samara, the Stranger, one of the world's Wanderers.

The Riding Officers talked among themselves and as Samara stood apart from the seated men, she made no attempt to hear their conversation. At the moment her chief concern was the occasional mention of Alexi. Just how much they had all, including the Justice of the Peace, involved her with Marika's son, she could not be sure. She had met him on the beach last night, but she was certainly not involved in whatever he and Dilys were about. Would they all give her a chance to say so in a court? She had very little confidence that they would. Too many of the Romany had discovered otherwise.

Several times the officers looked back at her. Their interest was furtive, as though they didn't trust her but were fascinated all the same.

The idea had been with her most of her life. These creatures were sexually drawn to her, but not at all the way they would be drawn to a supposedly virginal Christian girl. Their contempt for her people, combined with their obvious desire to possess her, seemed hypocritical in every respect.

But her thoughts lingered on the magistrate as she

163

heard the housekeeper in the hall exchange words with a male servant outside the open doors of the salon. Then the woman looked in at the officers.

"Sir Anthony will join you very—" As the front opened and then slammed shut, she curtsied in that direction, informing her employer, "The officers and their prisoner are in the salon, sir."

"A little late, but we'll see."

Samara knew that voice and resented her rising excitement as she heard it.

The four men got up, saluted Sir Anthony, and the young officer pointed out, "We have a gypsy prisoner here, as ordered. The only one we could find, and since the case involves an abduction in this region . . ."

Sir Anthony nodded gravely without looking at Samara. "Very proper. But was there a witness to any discussion between the prisoner and the gypsy Alexi?"

"Well, sir, we will know better when she is stripped and searched. They always carry a weapon."

Samara caught her breath but managed to show none of her panic. She remembered all too well the sharp and useful little knife they would find rolled in her sash.

Sir Anthony studied her. He asked finally, "What do you say to that, miss?"

The men exchanged glances. They couldn't recall ever calling a gypsy 'miss'. As for Samara, she snapped, "I would not suggest that search be attempted, sir."

Sir Anthony looked as if he might smile, but

164

instead pursued an observation he had already silently made.

"It would seem there is one chair missing."

The young officer raised his eyebrows and the others seemed puzzled. One of them who did not understand the allusion to the standing prisoner said quickly, "Your housekeeper made us very comfortable, sir. Would you care for us to quiz the prisoner on the matter of her acquaintance with the kidnapper Alexi?"

"No. I will attend to that. Thank you, gentlemen. You have been very helpful. We should find my ward in a matter of hours at the latest."

"But, Sir Anthony," the young officer protested as the others began to shuffle out in puzzlement, "we must rescue the young lady at once."

"Certainly. That is our intention."

So the little witch had run away with Alexi after all! And what has this to do with me? Samara asked herself. Sir Anthony must know she would not abduct the outrageous Dilys, whatever her private feelings about the girl.

The young officer stopped to suggest, "If you do not learn the truth from this woman, sir, it will take much longer. I mean to say, it will be disastrous if Miss Dilys is not returned to you until – er – after the night has passed, so to speak."

"Every vessel along the coast has been warned," the magistrate said stiffly. "And I am setting out this hour to bring her back myself."

"Ay, sir, but—" another officer began in the doorway.

"Enough!" Sir Anthony said. "I have my ward's welfare very much in mind."

The young officer shrugged at the others and Sir Anthony raised his voice. "Mrs Powell, see the officers out."

The doors into the hall had been left ajar and the housekeeper stood there as if by magic. As they left, the young officer stopped to remind him, "Naturally, we will have the coast watched. The cabin boy on the *Antelope* swears the gypsy was refused passage. He went on to a small coaster. Another gypsy would probably know what he did when he reached some little port. Good-day, sir."

When they were alone Sir Anthony reached into his jacket and took out a folded piece of creamy paper.

"I think you are entitled to see this."

She accepted the paper from him and read, taking care not to let her hands shake. It was so frighteningly like the amoral and irresponsible girl she had begun to know as Dilys Linden.

'My dear Cousin Anthony,

You must forgive our passion which drives us to do this thing, though it may shock you at first. We've run away to live in glorious freedom. We will die if we cannot be together forever.

Your friend, Samara, and now ours, the blessed creature, says if we are not together our lives will be disasters. She has the power to see things, you know.

166

Forgive her, and remember, she helped us for your sake as well as ours.

We love you. Some day we will meet again, in happiness.

Your Cousin Dilys Linden'

Samara folded the letter again and returned it to him, proud that she did not outwardly reveal the shock of this lie.

"What do you intend to do with me about these lies, sir?"

She wished she could read his face. She was used to this sardonic, rather hard look she remembered when he accused her in Heaton Clough. But until now it had always been possible that he was not quite as hard as he seemed.

"I suppose I could turn you over to your friends, the Riding Officers."

"To strip and search me?" She was proud of standing up to him.

"If you keep treating this so lightly, I'll strip and search you myself, you witch."

She felt better. Whatever his voice, something in his eyes excited and encouraged her. He would not turn her over for examination and trial.

Her manner softened. "If I swear to you I know nothing of their flight, can I not be going on my way to Dorset?"

"Certainly not. I'm not – the law is not through with you yet. I am looking for a gypsy and I haven't anyone but you at hand who thinks like a gypsy . . . What the devil is wrong with your face?"

She had forgotten until he pinched her chin with his thumb and forefinger.

"What happened? Your cheek is red as fire."

She hoped she had seen the last of the Riding Officers and said, "I tripped over a cobblestone."

"You are lying. Who did that?"

"It was nothing. The accounts are closed. I kicked him hard across the thigh."

He looked shocked and for an instant she wondered if she had made her case worse, but then, suddenly, he began to laugh.

"My friends who took you in charge, of course."

She grinned, though it hurt to do so.

He shook his head. "The poor fools. They had no idea they were taking a tigress into their hands."

"It doesn't matter. If you will only let me go on to Dorset."

He had reacted so well she thought things were looking up and was jolted when she saw that light in his eyes again, half-teasing, but undeniably firm.

"What? After you sent those brats on their way and expect me to believe it? No, indeed! You are going to use your wiles and find that gypsy lover for me."

Fifteen

S amara gave this remark a long sigh of boredom. "Alexi is not— But I won't argue the point. Would I demand more than my rights if I asked whether I may have a salve or basilicum powder for my wrists?"

Frowning and clearly embarrassed, he took one of her hands up, and examined it with surprising gentleness.

"Damn them! I didn't want this at all." He looked up from her fingers, saw her faint smile, and insisted in a tone almost boyish, "Well, I didn't, you know. I'll ring for Mrs Powell to attend you and meanwhile our heathen smuggler should be brought to us."

The housekeeper arrived so quickly Samara suspected she had been waiting outside one of the salon doors, listening. It didn't matter. The woman was apparently used to attending the abrasions of prisoners brought in for examination.

Having finished her work in a satisfactory manner the woman reminded her employer, "The seamen are waiting in your office, sir. Shall I send them in?"

Sir Anthony looked at Samara, saw that she was

satisfied with the simple medical attention, and said, "Certainly."

Two men came into the salon, one of them probably Irish, who grinned at Sir Anthony and put two fingers to his black beret in a salute.

"Ay, Sir. We're here. I don't speak his talk, but I'd a notion it was what you'd be wanting. His name is Cesare."

The other was clearly a Romany, very dark, his curly black hair standing out around his big hat. He was looking sullen, almost threatening, which Samara recognised as his protective shield in facing the Gentile magistrate.

"Well?" Sir Anthony asked abruptly. "What does he say about that rogue and my ward?"

The gypsy's startling black eyes looked out from under his wide-brimmed black hat, first at the magistrate, then at Samara, and he was clearly puzzled by her racial appearance.

In the argot of his Romany band, throwing in a descriptive remark now and again English, he demanded, "Are you one of them? You sell a true Rom to our enemies?"

Samara shook her head.

His eyes opened wider. "You do not betray me to them? I've done nothing but they will not believe."

"They will if I say so. Where was the Romany boy taking the Christian girl?"

"I don't betray him. It was the girl who insisted. She said they would pay well to the master of the ship."

Samara glanced at Sir Anthony who was watching

the gypsy carefully. He understood some of this and dismissed the last comment. "They will say anything to avoid punishment. Ask him where the gypsy was taking his prisoner."

She bit her lip. "She was not his prisoner . . . Very well." She returned her attention to the gypsy. "Where were they going?"

The gypsy shrugged. "He was not guilty. She wanted to go. The big two-master was on its way to Spain. But they wanted to leave at a port where they could take a coach to Genoa in the Italian States."

Sir Anthony groaned as Samara repeated the port to him. "Why Genoa?"

She asked the gypsy, "Are you sure they wanted to go to Genoa?"

The gypsy acted as though this were the most natural destination in the world.

"It was on the way to Rome."

Both Sir Anthony and Samara echoed: "Rome!"

"Of course. Is not Genoa on the way to Rome? The female said she must live in a palace for a time, and someone said Rome had many palaces." He added helpfully, "The female said they would have much money."

Samara saw that Sir Anthony understood. He said, "The rubies, of course." He took a deep breath. "Well, then, it's off to Genoa; if she doesn't stay there, it's Rome next, I see."

The Irish sailor asked, "Is the gypsy free to go, sir? He needs the work. He wants the money to get home to Devon. He has a family."

171

"I wish to God *I* didn't! Yes. He can go. But I'll need you to find us a fast ship."

"Well, sir, there's nothing registered at the Customs House at this hour. But there was a four-master in Dover last week. Looked mighty powerful."

"Do what you can, Jes."

When Samara was alone with Sir Anthony and having given some thought to the fate of his ward, she ventured now, "Would you consent to their marriage? Nothing else seems possible."

He was still looking after the departed sailors.

"Good God! What a solution! To have one of my family united to such a creature. A kidnapper and a thief. There would be no life whatever. They have nothing in common."

It was not as if such remarks, dragged out of the depths of his real feelings, had been new to Samara. But still she shuddered.

"Yes. It would be no future for Alexi either. He could never be genuinely accepted again in the band. How would he survive?"

He turned to her.

"He could live very nicely on the money from the ruby set."

She took this without revealing any anger or resentment. There was no time for that.

"Surely, with your influence, you can bring her back? And money would get a response. Since the wars, I'll wager the French and the Italian States and all the war-torn provinces would do almost anything for money."

172

"Depressing thought. That child with her entire future ahead being bargained and fought over!" He slapped the credenza near his hand, making her jump.

She considered all the possibilities and asked, "You did send men after them, I trust? I can't imagine how that would serve, but they might—"

He admitted, "My only hope, really. A naval friend of mine. He sailed for the Mediterranean at noon today. They touch at Naples, the Kingdom of the Two Sicilies. And Rome is not far from there. And two of the officers formerly with the Customs House took the Calais packet today. But they will reach Italy, and Genoa in particular, only after travelling the length of France."

He slapped the top of the credenza again, shrugged and seemed to pull himself together.

"Well, I have one or two ideas. They are far more likely than a few officers riding off in all directions through lands full of brigands, bandits, vagabond gypsies, soldiers from half a dozen Italian armies, not to mention some derelict French soldiers."

She had been considering his personal situation and reminded him suddenly, "You cannot possibly go through the different states of Italy, with all those different rulers, letting them see you as yourself, a British veteran, a rich man, and a magistrate. Most of them must have been on the emperor's side before Waterloo."

He was annoyed at this reflection on his courage.

"Shall I try for a bodyguard, a company of half-pay soldiers to Genoa and beyond?"

173

She pretended to be amused. She knew how concerned he was over the fate of his ward; the more negative the situation looked, the less likely the solution would come.

"Not if you seem to have nothing worth taking."

His eyes brightened. He began to study her.

"A gypsy, in fact."

"Take extra clothing for the countryside, the woods, all the places where renegades and other rogues are waiting."

"Good Lord! It will take me for ever to fight my way through that."

She admired his assumption that he actually could fight his way through the dangers of the ungoverned Italian states.

"The vagabond look would be a last resort, at certain places. My people have had to rely upon cunning all their lives. It's a pity you haven't a gypsy's cunning."

"A gypsy's cunning," he repeated. He had not stopped looking at her, and with a smile added, "You are the only gypsy I know."

"Oh, rubbish! Get that fellow who told you about Alexi and Miss Linden. Or – anyone."

"I prefer you."

She said firmly, "I am not for sale."

She did not like his confident look. "Haven't you ever wanted to see the world of your ancestors? Think what you will miss if you go to Devon and—"

"Dorset."

He waved his hand. "You may never have another chance. If you are afraid of me—"

174

"Certainly not!"

He laughed, enjoying himself. "You will be my gypsy. What do you call a Gentile friend who defends you?"

"A *gadjo*."

"I am your *gadjo*. You are Princess Samara of your own band, searching for your brother Alexi who is in trouble over a – whatever you call us."

"A *goy*?"

He wrinkled his nose. "Well, something of the sort. But you have a motive to be with me."

She thought of those tentative dreams she had in Yorkshire. Never again was there likely to be such a chance. The danger only made it more attractive.

As for her personal relations with Sir Anthony, they would depend upon circumstances and emotions. Her own. There were moments when her body was intensely drawn to him. But not if it made her a slave to her own desires. Or his.

She was not afraid of him. She was, perhaps, more afraid of herself. Besides, she could always use that little knife in her sash either to protect herself or him or both of them against the dangers of the search.

Sir Anthony had made up his mind and was very much in command of this expedition to rescue Dilys Linden from the monstrous abductor, Alexi. He called the old man Samara recognised as the coachman, ordered him to go down to the stables and prepare for a quick trip to Dover.

"We leave at once," he called after the coachman and then congratulated Samara on being thoroughly

175

packed. He added, "You may leave that dreadful wardrobe you wore on the mail coach. You will soon be Princess Samara when we touch port."

Though she always felt more like herself in her gypsy entertainer's costumes, she did not take his instructions too literally and when he had left the salon to pack, she put her best costumes and travel clothing into the portmanteau, having thrown out the rest.

There was a bandeau she often used when riding the wagons with Marika and Stefan. It was decorated with bright, small brilliants. It would serve to anchor her uncontrolled hair.

In a few minutes, half-hidden by the heavy drapes, she changed to a black and gold satin gown she used when she was appearing but not reading the cards. It was not noticeably faded.

When Sir Anthony came back with a battered case, he looked her over with flattering interest.

"Princess, you do me an honour. Give me that portmanteau and we'll be off."

He said it as if it were the simplest event of the day. She did not argue with him about it. The more she thought of the journey ahead, the more fascinated she became though, as usual, she tried to hide her feelings.

"You do know the dangers," he reminded her.

"You forget. I spelled them out carefully to you, sir."

"Very true. I haven't forgotten."

As they were leaving the house, she said, "Let's hope Miss Linden returns safely with you."

"Yes. We must include that, damn it!"

She remarked, "It's fortunate you never had any children."

His eyebrows raised. "You treat me as though I were in my dotage. What makes you think it is too late for me?"

"Some theories are too wild to dwell upon. Shall we go on?"

He gave her a heavy frown and informed her, "I'll probably throttle you before we return."

Sixteen

D over proved more hospitable then Sir Anthony's little town and before Samara was ready for it, she was helped out of the rocking dory and into the waist of a Spanish schooner. The ship's master agreed to make a stop out in the roads of a Basque port above the Spanish Coast.

Sea voyages were something of a mystery to Samara. Her memory of an Irish Sea crossing when she was just under five had faded during the moorland years since.

Sir Anthony, with his experiences in Spain during the war, was soon discussing the problems of his journey with Captain de Planna. The Spaniard knew him from frequent voyages during the war when his ship had carried men like Anthony Linden on secret missions between their countries.

He had little to add to the common gossip about conditions since the Peace that followed Waterloo, but he was shocked to hear that Sir Anthony intended to make the trip overland to Genoa and perhaps further into Italy.

"By sea, señor. There can be no doubt. You fetch up at one of those villages in Portugal or remain with us

179

until we dock and take a quick sloop, for example, and head for Naples, then Genoa."

Sir Anthony reminded him, "The trouble is, we are trying to stop this gypsy with my ward. They intend to take the shore route."

The captain shook his head.

"Not so, señor. Have you not heard of the brigands on those Italian mountain roads?"

Sir Anthony said drily, "I imagine you are aware of the Barbary pirates who prey on the ships off Lombardy and Tuscany."

The Spaniard shrugged. "It is in the hands of the Good God, señor, which danger you prefer."

Sir Anthony laughed. "Thanks. You are encouraging, my friend."

Samara was at first intrigued by the magic of a wooden vessel sailing out across the eternally angry waters of the Channel and not sinking. But this awe and curiosity began to fade as the waters grew rougher.

By late afternoon, hearing crewmen gamble on how rough the Bay of Biscay might be, despite the calm weather, Samara lost interest in the magic she had felt at seeing sloops, schooners and great, square-rigged four-masters bound homeward Britain and the Americas. There were too many near-misses in these crowded waters.

Worse than that. A strange malady she was beginning to suffer from became evident. It was an unsettled stomach. She couldn't understand that and it was very annoying. She was almost never sick.

In Samara's presence the captain had invited Sir

Anthony to his tiny cabin to dinner. Then, noticing the magistrate glance significantly at Samara, the captain included her with an "Of course" in his fair English.

The idea nauseated her and she was forced to refuse on the grounds that she had dined before they left Sir Anthony's house. It was a humiliating lie, to say the least.

Sir Anthony managed to conceal his smile and took her arm, much against her will. In what passed for their galley, whose odours only increased her nausea, he asked the lean, imperious-looking cook for some kind of liquid in a mug. Samara thought it was all she needed to complete the disaster, but he held the mug to her lips and she was forced to drink.

"What is it?" she gasped, choking on the liquid.

"A form of lime juice. Prevents scurvy."

She reminded him, "I don't have scurvy."

"Drink."

It was not quite as odious as she had thought at first.

Best of all, something about the juice was a blessing to her stomach. After a careful survey of his patient Sir Anthony decided she was safely out of danger and took her back up on deck, though neither of them made the journey without swaying to the roll of the ship.

Later, Samara decided to be sensible and eat lightly of the Spanish beef stew after Sir Anthony urged her, reminding her that they might not find any edible meals until they reached the French chateau of some wartime friends of his.

When Samara heard the captain and Anthony discussing the problem of her sleeping quarters, she found it ridiculous.

"I will sleep somewhere on deck, out of the wind, if I may borrow a heavy coat or a blanket. I am more comfortable in the out-of-doors," she told Anthony.

He was amused but could not see its practicality.

'You'll take your orders like any other crew member. I order you – take the captain's cabin when he offers it to you."

It was absurd and impractical but though the idea of obeying anyone, much less Sir Anthony, was madly annoying, she said nothing. The sea was not her province and she was technically Captain de Planna's guest.

How Marika would laugh at that!

She took the bed, but not being sure who might enter the tiny cabin at any hour of the night, she undressed only long enough to wash, using very little of the pan of water. She was at least aware that water on board ship was scarce and should be carefully husbanded.

She slept intermittently, waking every time barefooted seamen went running along the decks in the rising wind and voices sang out words incomprehensible to Samara. She wondered where Sir Anthony was at this hour and whether he was comfortable. He was probably used to a good deal more elegance than her own easy life of freedom.

At dawn she began to wonder what this journey would lead to. She was more excited than worried. If they didn't locate Dilys and Alexi at the first port, they might be occupied for weeks. But at least it would give her glorious memories of dangers defeated. There were few times when she really felt the breath of danger or possible death.

Long ago she had taught herself that being alone meant she need never depend upon all the weak, changeable creatures who made up the world around her in Heaton Clough.

Thinking over the possible dangers ahead, she could think of none that she was afraid to face. She wouldn't like to be killed, or badly injured, but those were dangers about which the Tarot could be counted on to warn her.

Besides, they could happen to anyone. Life was a chancy matter.

As soon as light came into the cabin, she used what remained of last night's water, washed and dressed as rapidly as possible and went out on the heavy deck. Seeing her look around with interest, one of the sailors, who spoke a fair, colloquial English, informed her that Biscay was in trouble again.

"The waters hereabouts, always the same, señorita. But you are a good sailor. It is not always so. I lived in Cordova as a boy. I know your people. They came to Cordova. Dancing bears and beautiful fortune-tellers and tumblers. I used to see them walk about on long, wooden stilts under the tents on rainy nights, you understand."

It was good to encounter a Gentile who had normal, pleasant contacts with her people.

In the end the good-looking young Spaniard asked if

183

she would see what the Tarot had to say about himself and a merchant's daughter in Seville who loved him, but only from afar. The girl was not permitted to be alone.

Amused and pleased, she knelt and spread her Tarot cloth in the lee of the galley, with the young Spaniard leaning over her shoulder, his gentle, sad eyes hopeful, when Sir Anthony came by and declared he would stay to see how the Spaniard's love affair would turn out, according to the Tarot.

Sir Anthony went on as an afterthought: "If, of course, you prefer the Tarot cards to breakfast . . ." He closed two fingers around the nape of her neck, but his touch was mischievous and she laughed.

"I didn't know you believed in the cards."

"Oh, señor," the young Spaniard put in, shocked. "It has been proven. The truth is in the cards."

Sir Anthony only laughed at this, adding the dubious advice, "Hurry and satisfy Fernando or the hard tack will grow cold."

This was not encouraging and Samara shuffled the cards half a dozen times. She knew Sir Anthony was amused and could not take any of her work seriously but she ignored that.

She explained about the sailor's past, as seen first, and then the present, and at last, his future, which began to excite him. What she read in the cards about his past had surprised her. He said he came from a family of conquistadors but was himself illegitimate. She mentioned the difficulties but Fernando was confident.

"We need not think about the past," Anthony said. "It is no concern of ours."

At which point Fernando objected, "But the gypsy knew before I told her. Now," he urged her, "the present again. More."

She turned up the ten of swords and once again found herself anxious to avoid the truth. The card told her that Fernando would probably be disappointed and that whatever this great concern of his, achieving it would be destructive to his happiness.

She passed over this with the cards' advice that his present dream of happiness would be replaced by the Star, which he drew next. Whether he won the fair lady, the next card did not indicate, but it promised happiness and a feminine influence that would be with him for his lifetime. Meanwhile, there would be a long wait.

Fernando was called to duty as Samara pointed out, before the half his fortune was told, but he had heard, or believed what he wanted to believe. He sped off along the deck, highly satisfied.

She looked up at Sir Anthony with a wry smile. "Some people believe what they want to believe."

"And do you?"

She knew he was making fun of her, but she said frankly, "I would be afraid to act against the cards."

"And there you have the truth about all these prophecies," he pointed out. He raised her head by putting his hand under her chin. "See if they can't prophesy something for you and me."

How strange that he could be wise in so many things

and hopelessly Gentile about the truth laid out before him in the Tarot deck!

It proved to her how far apart she and Sir Anthony were: a Gypsy and a Gentile. There could never be any real future that they might share. But Anthony was merely amused by her gullibility.

No matter. During the weeks they might be together – if they could stand each other that long – they might begin to appreciate the wisdom of the Tarot.

For the rest of the day and the morning following, she was kept busy reading what the Tarot cards had to say about those members of the crew who convinced themselves that the terrifying but almost dormant Inquisition should never hear about this tool of the devil.

On the day the ship anchored just outside a little French-Basque harbour to off-load a part of the cargo and the two passengers, Samara realised that her adventure of seeing the world was about to begin.

Anthony, for whom this area of Spain and France brought chiefly wartime memories, was more interested in Samara's reactions than in the real purpose of this journey. He wanted to find Dilys as soon as possible, or sooner, he added firmly, but meanwhile, there were other matters that occupied his thoughts.

Never having been on the Continent before Samara had not known what to expect and accepted the little village with interest. The stony path that was the leading street of the town looked somnolent and very Spanish, and bare-legged children played about the single wharf. There was little greenery and there were fewer females than she had expected.

Captain de Planna was in a hurry to be rid of the wool cargo and spirits from England and replace them with Spanish and Portuguese wines. While Sir Anthony questioned a sleepy lounger outside the local Mairie, Samara watched de Planna's ship sail off on its long voyage around Gibraltar to the Balearic Isles and Valencia. Then she turned to see what Anthony was about. The lounger had merely shrugged in answer to Anthony's question and as Anthony turned away, the fellow rattled off some unintelligible French, only one of whose words, '*le prefet*', was understandable. Evidently, the prefect was away in Toulouse.

Wandering out of a little cafe opposite the wharf were two men of middle age, one of whom wore a scarf tied around his head and reminded Samara of Marika's husband, Stefan, though he was not nearly so dark. The man left his friend and came down to the wharf to kick his boot against the load left by the Spaniards.

"Not yours, señor? Eh?"

Anthony was polite. "The card on the straw baskets reads 'Property of the Prefect.' The contents are not mine."

"*Ah, si.* The mistress of the prefect. Wine and spirits. A stout one, the prefect's lady. Not like this beauty, eh, señor?" His elbow indicated Samara.

Since Sir Anthony was clearly prepared to be insulted for her, Samara smiled at the man, whoever he was, and nodded. Anthony looked at her in surprise, then laughed and said to her in English, "Why don't you smile at me that way?"

"Ah, but I can be myself with you; isn't it so, sir?"

187

He said dubiously, "I understand you less every hour." He added on a different note, "I want to buy a vehicle of some kind and a strong horse. We must get to Genoa by one means or another."

He looked around the little village where a few men sauntered out of the other stone houses, including the building that bore the name of the Mairie and the local prefect.

A stout, jolly little Frenchman stood now in the open doorway of the prefect's office with a clay mug in one hand. Having satisfied himself of Anthony's identity, he tossed away the contents of the mug, making a sweeping gesture with it, then came bustling down the path to Sir Anthony.

"A friend of yours, I trust," Samara whispered.

Anthony gave her a look that was half-amused, but his reply was not entirely convincing.

"These postwar rogues are useful so long as our money holds. Many of them are half-pay officers making whatever they can, however they may."

The jolly little man reached them and threw himself into Sir Anthony's arms. His English was not the clearest but it was understandable for the most part.

"My good capitaine! Forgive me. You wished to see Monsieur le Prefet? But he is away at the moment."

"Not this time, Michel. I'm sure you will serve as well."

"Then how may I be of use to you?"

Anthony said, "I need supplies at once, my friend."

Michel was all smiles. He rubbed his palms.

"You have but to speak."

"A cousin of mine, my ward, has been abducted by a gypsy." He looked at Samara. "He is a member of a band from Ireland or England."

She nodded and Michel looked at her. She saw at once that he disliked her. Probably an old memory of gypsy thieving somewhere.

Michel cleared his throat and spat into the ground, just missing Anthony's boot.

"You are unfortunate there, monsieur. Some Spanish gypsies are encamped somewhere in the hills. But they will not let this woman of a different band pass them."

"Why not?" From Anthony's tone Samara suspected he did not believe Michel. At all events, it seemed unlikely that they should have an enmity toward Samara. There were seldom gypsy blood feuds in Samara's experience of the different bands.

But Michel apparently had his reasons for this comment.

"It may be the fault of the pair you mention. They came through the area the day before yesterday after being landed nearer the mountains."

"What have they done?" Anthony asked, prepared for anything.

"They were well treated, monsieur. Food and beds in the forest, and when they left they stole the leader's mule and cart. No one has caught them yet. I am told their destination was Genoa. If that failed them, they would go on down the Peninsula to Rome or Naples."

Anthony and Samara exchanged glances. "And one of the two was a gypsy?" Anthony asked.

Samara guessed at the excitement he was trying to hide.

"The young male, certainly. Not of their band, of course. And a thief, as one might expect. Either he or the young girl offered a precious jewel if they could be taken to a port and a sloop or a felucca to carry them to Genoa."

"A jewel. Yes, I can imagine," Anthony said. "And did they not pay?"

"What can you expect from a gypsy rogue? But heaven pity the next Gentile who asks a favour of them."

"Still," Anthony pursued the subject in a light, joking voice, "a little present, of gold perhaps, would soften them."

Michel looked around the area of the little village and then said casually, "There are far more useful men. I myself happen, by chance, to know some good fellows I would trust." He turned his attention back to Anthony, blinking innocently.

"How far away are your friends?" he asked.

Michel scratched his tousled head.

"Let me send to find them. Some may be nearer than even I know. They are hunting in the woods near the high road taken by the Toulouse public coach and others to the Gulf."

Samara thought Anthony had taken leave of his senses when he shook hands with Michel and paid for the use of a horse and cart which would serve to convey his ward's 'duenna' as they traced Alexi and his prisoner.

190

Michel looked over the dark and dangerous 'duenna', shook his head at the notion of trusting a genteel young female to the gypsy's care, and started away. He stopped seconds later and came back to suggest that a few florins or ducats or English pounds would soften the dispositions of his friends.

Anthony was nothing if not obliging.

"By all means. As soon as I have asked the advice of my bankers in Genoa."

After a slight hesitation, Michael agreed. "Just so, monsieur."

Probably they will cut our throats before we even reach Genoa, Samara thought. If Anthony was robbed of his money and credit, she would, without doubt, have to give them the money in her petticoat.

"Meanwhile," Anthony went on "I cannot wait. I will have the use of the horse and gig or whatever, until your friends meet us. You must describe to them the road we will take. I don't want to get myself lost in this area."

Michel patted the pocket of his jerkin absent-mindedly, caught himself at this gesture, and said in his jolly way, "Yes. I will describe your route to them. It should not be long. A very few hours. Certainly before dusk. I will send them off immediately."

A few minutes later one of the lounging men on the wharf had gone loping off, returning with a little carriage very like a gig, with a strong mare, better than one might have expected.

Sir Anthony, however, seemed unsurprised.

"This should serve, Michel. I'll need food for the trip. Can your town manage that, my friend?"

Michel looked as though about to shrug but Anthony poured a small handful of coins, English, French and Spanish, into his hand and Michel thought he could manage after all. As he walked off to arrange a basket for them, Samara was disapproving.

"They can't be real coins you gave him."

"The English coins are. The French and Spanish can't be worth much until the governments are more secure. Wars are hard on coinage, and even worse on paper money."

"Do you really believe that little man?"

He looked at her and smiled. "I don't believe you trust me."

She was ill-tempered because she thought his naïve belief in these rogues would get their throats cut. Unpleasant as this would be, she resented more her disappointment in his stupidity than the perhaps bloody result.

"You know quite well his friends will follow and rob us."

"I agree."

"But then . . . ?"

"Hush!"

He took the reins and examined them. They seemed satisfactory. He swung onto the seat of the gig and held out his free hand to bring Samara into the seat beside him. She felt very little more secure in joining him but he seemed confident. She could only hope for the best.

A few minutes later, Michel came out of the kitchen

house adjoining the Mairie. He went towards them carrying a Spanish woven basket and grinning as he assured them, shouting from beyond the wharf, "All serene, my friend. You will never forget this feast."

Samara shook her head. "I once saw a murderer being taken to trial in Leeds. He had killed his wife. He had a grin like that."

"Good God!" Anthony exclaimed, but he did not smile.

Seventeen

S ince her companion was embarked on some folly, Samara remembered Marika's way with Stefan and said nothing, but made plans for instant action when necessary.

Sir Anthony gave the mare the office to start while he looked down from the cart and thanked the waving Michel again.

"Thanks, friend. I vaguely recall this road. With care, and perhaps a little help from your men, I can reach the Toulouse diligence if it is running again."

Michel was nothing if not enthusiastic.

"Better yet, monsieur. Our men might escort you around the Gulf to the Italian border. And you will find Genoa in no time. *Bon chance.*"

Anthony called back, "And luck to you, my friend."

The mare trotted forward amiably.

As soon as they were out of Michel's hearing, Anthony grinned at Samara.

"And now we go to perdition as directed by our friend Michel."

"Very likely."

He did not seem moved by her sullen voice. She was

surprised at his easy nature when they should be looking for a way out of this morass.

When they had lost all sight of the half-civilised little port behind them, Anthony remarked in a friendly way, "I do believe this has been our first quarrel."

"What? We've done nothing but quarrel since we met."

He dismissed this easily. "But I can quarrel with my love, of all people. Love and hate? Very close. You were afraid you might love me that night in my bed."

"Ridiculous. Part of the time I hated you."

"Of course. Positive proof." He slapped her hand. The mare looked back but saw no danger and went trotting on.

Samara thought this an absurd conversation when they were in danger. But he went on, "If you had said you did not like me, you'd have given me something to worry about. I may hate you sometimes but I think I loved you the moment you bit me."

It was no use. She could not be angry at this moment. He was too ridiculous. This dangerous journey and her companion were the very things she had wanted in life. Now they were here, she would enjoy them. Avoiding an apology for her bad temper, she asked,

"What may we expect? Dare I hope you have a plan?"

"Several."

She groaned but had to smile. "We fight off Michel's jolly friends?"

He had begun to look around more carefully as the

road narrowed into little more than a dusty trail wandering up slightly through a dark, thickly forested area.

He said, "Do you gypsies have any signs to mark trails for others in your tribe?"

"In our band. Yes."

"Keep a sharp eye out for anything that may seem to you like a sign."

She was glad to be kept busy.

Since the Romany band was evidently here in these woods for the winter, there were very likely signs to tell other Romany that it was a safe place.

Why Sir Anthony wanted to find an encampment of her kind of people, she wasn't sure, considering that they had been cheated and robbed by Alexi and the *goy*, Dilys Linden. Unless Samara was very convincing, they might despise her and Sir Anthony.

"Find anything?" Anthony asked, frowning into the forest ahead of them. The air had acquired a dusty late-afternoon hue.

Carefully examining the bushes and trees beyond, she did not answer at once but finally made out something small and red fluttering in the bole of a tree.

"That leaf may be a sign if it's marked correctly."

There seemed to be no path near it but Anthony signalled the mare to stop and with the reins in hand he looked over the tree and then awaited Samara's judgement. Luckily, she knew at once.

"Yes. It must be what I've been looking for."

A twig had pierced the leaf and appeared like a

straight forward sign but Samara pointed out, "It's the back of the leaf stuck through the twig."

He took it from her but couldn't see the difference this made until she explained.

"When we have no Gentile money and need a decent dress, we turn one of ours inside out and with a bit of sewing, make it less faded. But you see the leaf here is still the underside."

"And—?"

"There is a trail somewhere nearby but it is to the left, not the right. A Gentile would take the wrong direction for many minutes. Or hours."

"Crafty rascals. They don't trust anyone. I really can't blame them for that. Shall we try the left trail when we reach the cut-off?"

He started to lead the mare into the bush area, remarking, "When the mare can't make a further trek, do we carry her or just abandon her? As for that comfortable plank seat we've been sharing, we can always kindle a fire with it."

She laughed. "Let's try and see. Don't forget. An entire band of gypsies with their worldly goods came through here, or somewhere very like this."

He took her word for it and led the horse into the copse without breaking an inordinate amount of twigs and boughs.

He soon found she was right. They got into the copse without leaving too many signs of their passing in this area where the evening breeze would soon sweep away much of the broken twigs.

There was a definite trail less than a mile into the

forest and Anthony was pleased to tell Samara, "Your people ought to have been used more during the wars. They would have cut our work of crawling over Spain."

She reminded him, "When the Gentiles have wars, we know where we are safest – somewhere else."

He agreed. "Very wise."

The mare proved a little irritable after several miles and Samara sympathised, sharing the animal's feelings, but by this time she would have died rather than admit it to her companion, who was obviously used to lengthy campaign marches.

There were occasional sounds around them, but at a distance, and Anthony pointed out the fact that the sounds were on their right. Soon they died away. Obviously, whoever they were, they had read the gypsy signs wrong.

Except for the stars and the rising moon, the forest was dark now and small noises here and there suggested that the travellers had unseen company around them.

Anthony stopped in a little glade, looked around, considered the dappling rays of moonlight on every side, and took a full breath.

"At this hour it appears we are far too late for dinner, so it will have to be supper. Shall we see what friend Michel has provided us with?"

"Nothing poisonous, I hope."

"Not at least until they've gotten the rest of my money."

Hungry as she was it relieved her that Anthony took

care of the mare first while she laid out the blankets for a few hours' sleep.

He teased her about her own previous choices of bedding and comfort.

"I suppose you will be perfectly happy with the spiders and crawling things on the ground."

"Perfectly," she agreed. "More so than that awful bed in your house, like a great heap of feathers ready to bury you."

He laughed but confessed this had often been his own view, especially after he came home from the wars.

"But I found I could grow accustomed to comfort, if I must."

With the mare combed, curried, washed and generally made comfortable, Samara and Anthony settled down to see what Michel had acquired for them.

"We could have used a fire," Anthony apologised, "but we will eat – and sleep – better if there are not more signs of us about than necessary."

This was no disappointment to Samara. She had never expected comfort on this journey and was more than pleased with the arrangements. The chicken roasted over coals and probably intended for Michel's dinner was cold, of course, and very skinny, but not too many people or animals in this vicinity had been well-fed during the last few years.

Not at all sure whether they would find hospitality anywhere else for some time, Samara hungrily eyed the chicken, the broiled meat of a rabbit, and the baked vegetables from some root cellar.

A Splash of Rubies

The Spanish wine was welcome, though Anthony said he would give a hundred guineas for a drop or two of French brandy. Nevertheless, she noted that he drank the wine without being forced to do so.

There were noises all around them but they were no worse than the small sounds Samara was used to on the chilly moors of Yorkshire. Even the mare neighed once or twice and made Samara remember the soft *whiffer* of the friendly and inquisitive sheep on the moors.

"We'd better take our turn on the watch," she suggested as Anthony was rubbing the mare down again while Samara gathered up the remains of the food.

Like Samara Anthony spoke in little more than a whisper, listening every minute or so, but now he said, "Rubbish! We both have sharp ears."

She did not know how she expected to sleep or how long, but it became evident that they would lie on one blanket spread over the dusty ground amid the prickle of twigs and pebbles. However, the wine and the long hike over unfamiliar ground had tired her, and after the removal of the bad-weather pattens from her feet, she was half-asleep when she curled up on the extreme edge of the blanket, wishing she had unwrapped her all-weather cloak in which her clothes were bundled. She might at least have used it comfortably now to cover her fast-chilling feet.

Almost immediately she sat up again and said, "May I ask you a question about our destination?"

"Certainly. I thought you knew. We are on our way

201

to rescue an idiotic child from her abductor." He patted the mare murmuring, "Good girl. You've done well."

She lost her patience.

"I mean, why are we in this forest at this hour waiting for some rogues to rob us and then cut our throats?"

He gave her one of those puzzled looks she could imagine even if it was almost invisible in the moonlight.

"But I thought you guessed. We are hoping to encounter some of your gypsy friends whom I will bribe to get us to Genoa. This, of course, without my friend Michel and his cut-throats to know my plan. It occurs to me that your gypsies, above all, would love to have me arrest and bring that bastard Alexi to justice. You've no objection to that, I hope?"

He knew quite well that she didn't want Alexi executed, which would certainly be his fate in an Italian court, but she did not say so now. That would have to wait until they had captured the stupid boy.

"As a payment for the help of your gypsies, I will, of course, repay them in honest coin."

"Suppose they decide to cut your throat instead?"

"What!" He was almost horrified. "Not when you speak up for me. You've always let me understand your people are decent, harmless citizens, honest to the core."

She had certainly never said that! As usual, he was making a fool of her. She was torn between gritting her teeth and laughing, but ended by slamming herself back down on the blanket and closing her eyes.

Despite their dubious safety, Samara was nearly asleep when she, who never shared her bed with anyone, suddenly became aware that her privacy had been invaded.

Sir Anthony lay down beside her on the under-blanket but did not touch the top blanket, most of which she had left for him. He lay there with his eyes open, staring up at the night sky.

She said finally, "It's growing cold. Half the blanket is yours."

He chuckled, turned his head to look at her and then admitted, "I didn't like sleeping on the bare ground when I fought the French and to tell the truth, I still haven't caught the trick of it. The end of my spine objects to it."

She smiled to herself and pushed the top blanket toward him. "You British are so delicate. I am surprised the French didn't beat you."

"They nearly did. Ask Wellington."

He muttered something, leaning on one shoulder, while he stared into her face. He was suddenly so close she thought she could see either the starlight or simply anger reflected in the pupils of his eyes.

"I called you a bitch once, didn't I?"

"Probably." She remembered two or three others who had called her that but they had not excited her. She usually despised them. They hadn't made her pulses race as this teasing devil did. His mouth was so near she could have bitten him. While she wondered what would happen if she did, she felt his mouth hard upon hers, as if he would draw her own emotions into his own.

All too easily he conquered her quick resistance with his physical strength.

The night wind came up while they lay together, their lips hot upon each other's body and he laughed softly when she murmured, "This cold night – strange. I'm so warm . . ."

He whispered with his mouth near her ear, "We will share it. Whenever I see you, I am hot with wanting you. Show me you do love me a little."

The heat of their bodies made them forget the world around them.

At last she fought to release herself and there were several minutes before the forest and the night took over and her flesh cooled.

He took her to him more gently. "Let me keep you warm."

But as the mare neighed across the glade she reminded her companion, "We are disturbing the mare."

"Damn the mare!"

She laughed softly and reached for the second blanket as she suggested, "Shall we share it?"

They had both enjoyed the violent tussle that left them breathless but contented and somewhat to her surprise, she went to sleep with her body tucked close to his.

It was still dark but close to dawn when she felt the pressure of his hand over her mouth. She was startled to wakefulness but knew at once what had happened. Somewhere, evidently not too far away, twigs snapped and she heard a human voice curse.

She stared up into Anthony's eyes. He whispered, "Michel's men," but she had guessed that at once. She sat up silently, straightening her skirts and reached behind her to her sash. The knife remained there, rolled up. She took it out, stuck it up her buttoned sleeve, and was ready. Beside Anthony was a buckskin container which he had taken already from his luggage. He slipped out a large, serviceable pistol. At least they were not caught entirely unprepared.

At that moment the mare neighed and in the grey light of dawn Samara saw Anthony's face, hard and very much aware as booted steps crushed the bushes at the far end of the glade and a scrawny little man came into view. He had teeth too big for his thin mouth and reminded Samara of some night creature with glittering little eyes. She half-expected him to rise on his toes and hiss at her and Sir Anthony.

Anthony's arms were crossed in what appeared to be a nonchalant attitude.

The toothly little creature said, "You put us to a deal of trouble, *Anglais*. If you'd simply emptied your pockets to us on the road as you were meant to do, like other *Anglais* who come ashore into our hands, you'd have gone your way with very little lost except your English dignity."

Anthony grinned. "Good of you to make yourself known. We had nearly a company of men out beating these hills for you eight or ten years ago. They missed you every time. My congratulations. But of course, we were younger then. You were called – what was it? – something appropriate. An oily serpent. Something like that."

The wizened fellow with the rifle pointed at Anthony ignored this. Without looking back he called to another pair of rogues making their way out of the forest behind him: "Pierre! Lenard! No more of this idiocy. The damned gypsies may take a notion to interfere. Search him."

Then he frowned at Samara standing across the glade.

"They said there was a gypsy with him." He gestured with his rifle. "Bind her hands. But don't get rid of her yet."

The big man in the long, heavy coat of a French foot soldier moved to Samara who was nervous but ready and looked to Anthony for an indication of his next move.

The big man had reached Samara and his heavy fingers raised her chin. He bawled out, "The gypsy bitch is worth saving for the night. Get on with it."

The third of the group, lean and very dark, possibly a Spaniard, crossed the glade to see what had aroused the big man's interest in the gypsy.

Their reptilian little leader ordered them to get to business. To encourage them he raised the rifle.

"Search the *Anglais*, you fools."

The Spaniard had turned toward Anthony when the heavy man reached for the neck of Samara's gown. She pulled back in revulsion and the neck of her bodice tore halfway down to her sash. She paid no attention to that but fingered the knife with all the strength in her hand as Anthony unfolded his arms. His heavy pistol was pointed not at the approaching Spaniard but at their leader whose rifle was suddenly aimed.

Too late. He fired but Anthony's aim was excellent and his timing better. The other two men, confused by the unexpected direction of Anthony's shot, spun around, the heavy man firing wide and the Spaniard running to his leader's aid.

The little man, looking puzzled, staggered and tried to raise the rifle but it fell from his slackened grasp and he collapsed to the accompaniment of the mare's neighing and stamping in panic.

Anthony threw himself down on the blanket and his buckskin bag, reaching over to get his hands on his second pistol.

The big man had recovered from his confusion and seized Samara, pulling her to him as a shield. With her small knife in her palm she turned the weapon inside his hand and stabbed into his palm. He screeched and let her go, moaning between curses. His own weapon dropped to the ground somewhere and he was concerned only for his bloody and damaged hand.

Before the Spaniard aimed at Anthony the latter fired his second pistol seconds before the Spaniard's weapon went off. The two sounds echoed through the forest. Samara looked around in panic, but the Spaniard's shot must have missed. He lay on the ground in a huddled mass.

Samara saw Anthony wave to her as if the bloody business happened every day.

He called, "Are you hurt?" She shook her head, too weak for an instant to reply. He called, "Thank God!" She pulled herself together and tucked the torn cloth of her bodice back into her sash.

Anthony looked down at the Spaniard, knelt and put his fingers against the man's throat and then told Samara, "Two of them are gone and the whining fellow you dispatched isn't in any shape to give us trouble."

He got up and suddenly muttered, "Christ!"

He took a step with an effort, looked down and shrugged. He kept coming toward Samara but there was no mistaking his limp. He reached Samara, felt her arms around him unexpectedly, and grinned.

"Brave soldier! At least, we can get back to our well-earned sleep when we've persuaded the mare to get us out of this—"

She shook her head but tried to be more casual than she was feeling.

"I'm afraid not. We may have lost more than the mare. Look around the glade. We have company."

Eighteen

The glade was encircled by six or seven men, some of them only half visible in the dawn. They were unquestionably Romany, most of them with their ink-black curls of hair half-concealed under brimmed black hats. Their pantaloons were old, faded, and darker than their strange, dark-gold flesh. Their homespun blouses were different colours, mended but still useful, and brightly cheerful when worn with their sleeveless jerkins.

Their only weapons seemed to be the knives they wore in leather thongs dangling on their hips and moving with every stride the men took. They were taking them now, closing the ring around Anthony while they avoided the two dead men and the groaning fat renegade. Their midnight-black eyes did not miss Samara as she moved among them to stand by Anthony. Not one of these captors said a word.

Anthony grinned at the gypsies but as he put his arm around Samara he asked her, "Just how friendly would you say they are?"

Nervous as she was, Samara felt better because she found his pretence of easy assurance admirable. It was far more comfortable than facing a dozen other sinister possibilities. She advised Anthony now: "Have a care what you say. At least find out if they speak English."

"True. I hoped to get help from them but not in a river of blood. If things grow violent, will you promise me to stand back?" His eyebrows went up as he added a second thought: "Unless you have another knife."

She almost laughed but knew that would be fatal to the dignity of the band. Although murder was least likely from them, they were very proud and might kill her to prove they were more dangerous than a woman and a *goy.*

She decided the tall, slightly greying man with the penetrating black eyes must be the Romany leader. She spoke to him in the accent of Marika's husband, Stefan, some of whose ancestors had escaped massacre in the Kingdom of the Two Sicilies and found their first refuge in Ireland.

"Forgive us for intruding, but a renegade from my band has abducted a child. This gentleman's ward."

The gypsy leader listened intently, saying only, "And then?"

She took a breath. His features did not look promising.

"We traced them here and the criminal had already taken her away. To these forests. He stole—" For a few seconds she hesitated, feeling it a betrayal of Marika and Stefan to entirely blame their son when she suspected the girl had so much to do with it. "He stole the jewels from the child's guardian. Here, according to the boast of the men in the port village, the criminal stole a horse and wagon from a band of Romany."

The gypsy leader glanced at his men, who had gathered closer.

"What will happen if he is captured and returned to England?" He had spoken suddenly in English and Anthony, who was putting most of his weight on his left leg, winced again and straightened up with an effort.

Samara looked down and cried out instinctively. Blood had seeped down from the calf of Anthony's right leg and into his boot. He dismissed this abruptly.

"A near-miss. If it were serious, I couldn't walk. Now, gentlemen, can we come to business?"

The gypsy leader ordered two of his men to remove the injured fat man still cradling his hand. His bulbous eyes stared wildly at the two silent gypsies who got him up under his arms.

"What'll you do with me? I've done nothing. Where are you taking me?"

The gypsy leader told Anthony, "We will leave him near the high road to the port. If he makes a report of us, he will be dead before the next sunrise. We have members of our band everywhere, so have a care. Does he understand me?"

There was no doubt the renegade understood.

"Cut his throat now," one of the gypsies called out in the Romany dialect, but he was ignored and the fat man was removed from the glade by pushes and shoves.

211

"The other two are dead," one of the gypsies announced, after examining them with the toe of his badly worn boot.

Meanwhile, Samara got out one of her head scarves and under Anthony's brisk instructions bound up the bloody, torn flesh where the shot had passed through, grazing the bone. Almost before she finished Anthony pulled away and started to stamp his foot to restore its normal use.

The pain of this movement made him swear and grit his teeth. One of the gypsies laughed but the leader said, "Be quiet, you fool! You want to be heard?"

"After our battle any listener must have overheard!" Anthony said. Then he was back to business. "Can you take us to the nearest town of any size? We must get to Genoa. I have reason to believe the gypsy – that is, the abductor – has taken my ward there."

"And with our nag and our horse cart," Another gypsy spoke in their dialect. "If this *goy* is going to get the thieving traitor hanged, I say let him get on with it."

The leader was thoughtful. He looked from Anthony to Samara, speaking in English. "We do not want the new government coming in to rout us out. We will be imprisoned or murdered. It is always the way of things, and worse since the war."

Anthony said, "I'm familiar with the justice in these parts. They were about to hang a ten-year-old boy, the last time I was here."

"First, we must see to Sir Anthony's injury," Samara put in. It was all very well to be bold and display his manliness, but she reminded them, "He won't get far this way."

"Don't interfere, damn it!" Anthony interrupted.

But the leader was already making arrangements. "We will leave you at some high road where the diligence or a mail coach passes by. But I must have your solemn oath that you will not betray our present location here in the forest."

Anthony started to speak, then turned to Samara.

"I can do no more than offer my oath. I swear by God Almighty I will not betray you."

She put out her hand, still stained with. Sir Anthony's blood. "I swear by my hopes for my people that I will not betray you."

She hoped the Englishman was sincere. She thought he was.

The leader took her hand.

In another minute the gypsies were clearing the glade and two of them went after the mare, whose panic during the gunshots had caused her to break her tether and get herself entangled in a thicket beyond. She was neighing mournfully but settled down when strong, useful hands freed her and brought her back.

Anthony patted and calmed the animal but saw that she was safe. He gave the tether to the gypsy leader.

"My ward and her abductor owe you a horse and a wagon. You look like a man who will care for her. She is yours."

The leader's serious, dark features yielded to a smile.

"It is fair. I will care for her. Sometimes I prefer animals to men."

"And I too," Anthony agreed. They shook hands in the English style.

As they started back through the forest following the light-footed mare and one of the gypsies, the others remained behind to bury the remains of the two dead renegades.

Anthony limped along but Samara was careful not to mention his injury. He took her hand after a few minutes, saying, "Here. Don't slip. You must be damned tired."

She reminded him, "I had excellent company." The squeezing of her fingers by his was the answer, that and his eyes, which told her he remembered.

The sadness crept in when, despite the warmth of his hand on hers, she knew her own life with him was only temporary. The passion, the danger, the excitement they shared would fade with the return to England.

The gypsies who had buried the two dead renegades and removed the third one, appeared presently to rejoin their companions. Their leader, who was thoughtful, as though he still was unsure of their safety, said nothing about his private thoughts and stopped to rest the mare. Though Anthony objected irritably, Samara suspected that his stop was also on Anthony's account. He offered the two visitors chunks of chewy black bread and water brought in mugs from a nearby stream.

Anthony limped over to the wagon to get a shirt out of his old valise and began to tear it in strips with his strong teeth. Samara helped him wash the wound and was about to take the cloth from him to bind the injury when the leader waved her away. He took his knife off the thongs dangling at his hip and Anthony approved what looked to Samara like a bloodthirsty operation. She was elbowed aside by one of the gypsies who reached for Anthony's thigh and held it as the leader cut away the torn flesh.

Anthony hissed as he drew in his breath but remarked to the leader with reasonable calm, "You've had experience, my friend."

The leader said, "It is sometimes necessary. Do not move."

Samara, who seldom showed much pity, winced as the leader removed the spent shot, but surrounded by the hardened gypsies and Anthony who had spent the last twelve years in a guerrilla war, the operation ended satisfactorily. She tried to be as calm as Anthony was. At the same time she was proud of her Romany people for their skills.

When it was over and Anthony was sweating in spite of the cool morning, they permitted her to wrap his thigh with strips of Anthony's shirts For an instant she felt almost noble. Then she caught Anthony's eye and saw his grin.

"That's my brave girl."

There was unmistakeable teasing in this, if not plain sarcasm, but he was entitled to any small amusement if it made him happy. She returned his grin.

Anthony tried out his bandaged leg by walking a couple of steps and assured the gypsy leader, "I could walk from here to Perpignian, or Nizza, when it comes to that. We are preventing you from your own duties, friend. If we could borrow back my horse and wagon, with one or two of your men to return them to you, we will pay you well, as soon as we get into the Italian States and I can exchange my money and credit."

One of the men objected and another one grumbled.

"They'll steal the mare and anything else. You know these whining *goys* when they are out of your sight. They'll steal anything they put their hands to."

At this opinion, surprising to Anthony especially, Samara and Anthony exchanged glances and both grinned. She knew she would remember the gypsy's accusation the next time Anthony had occasion to call her people thieves.

But the leader waved aside the gypsy's opinion and turned to Anthony.

"I have given it some thought. Your first suggestion was a good one. You will probably find your ward and the Romany in Genoa, Sir Anthony."

"Not if they went on at once."

The leader shook his head.

"The young lady insisted that she needed a fortnight in Genoa to purchase the materials for her marriage. Considerable, if the young lady does not exaggerate."

"In this case, she doesn't," Anthony said drily. "What did her lover – that is, her abductor – say to that?"

"He was opposed. He was afraid the young lady's guardian would kill him."

"I probably will. But she won the dispute, of course."

A *Splash of Rubies*

"Oh, yes. A very opinionated female, even for a *goy*." The leader added, "To get you to Genoa we can provide you with a team and wagon—"

"No, Luther! Nothing more to the *goy*," the toothy, husky gypsy objected. "They'll steal that too."

The leader contradicted him in his cool way. "Not if you ride with them, as Sir Anthony suggests. You will bring back the team and wagon, care for the team itself, and serve very well, Dominguez."

Anthony explained for the sake of the gypsy band, "As soon as I reach my English connection with the Italian brokers, I will pay you and your men what you feel the use of the wagon and team are worth."

"Fair enough, eh, Dominguez?"

Dominguez cleaned his teeth with his thumbnail and then shrugged. "If the others agree. Why do you not go yourself, Luther?"

The leader shook his head. "We can't trust the renegade with the stab wound. He may betray us in spite of the injury. We will have to move on."

Samara felt guilty, especially when the gypsies all looked at her, but Anthony reminded them, "My credit is good in some of the Italian States, so far as I know. And we will have friend Dominguez to see that we do not cheat you."

"We know that," Luther told him, speaking for men who might not entirely agree with him. "Some of our band came originally to Italy from Tripoli. Like Dominguez here. He escaped the police of the Two Sicilies and joined a brotherhood of our band. They all know Dominguez."

217

"Are we driving you out of your winter camp?" Samara asked.

"In the end, we will be paid," Luther assured her.

"I swear you will, on my honour," Anthony said, holding out his hand and receiving the gypsy leader's clasp in return.

Men were strange, Samara thought. She herself would never have considered her word sacred if so much was at stake.

She trusted the gypsy leader as a man of honour, surprising as it might be, but she emphatically did not trust the toothy Dominguez.

Among other points of interest, was the fellow to share the gypsy caravan with her and Anthony?

Nineteen

B efore Anthony and Samara could be on their way, every member of the band was given the right to vote. They seemed to take their cue from their leader, as if knowing his thoughts and understanding his intentions. Samara did not like this, but it was Sir Anthony's problem and she said nothing.

Having more or less gained a consensus, they agreed to send Anthony and Samara on their way with the good wishes of their leader, Luther. Even their accompanying spy, if that was his task in their company, agreed rather sourly to go along with them and return the wagon and horses plus the charges they would owe.

Anthony questioned the freedom of the gypsies with Dominguez, but Luther merely smiled and assured him that the 'fellow' valued his life and future.

"Whatever that might mean?" Anthony murmured to Samara, who did not like the idea any better but reminded him that Dominguez was no match for Anthony and herself.

Although Anthony laughed, he did not deny her remark.

Once they set off after receiving the reins of the

wagon and the two sturdy horses, the gypsy and Anthony took turns to drive and made a point of following the waters of the Gulf of Lions in exceedingly good time.

Only one thing chilled Samara. She still felt that the gypsy leader was far too sensible to send only one of his band with a Gentile who owed them for the loan of one of their wagons and the money for its use.

But it was not her concern, so long as Anthony's injury seemed to be healing and he was enjoying himself. Since they were living the very life that she had always dreamed about, she didn't want to interfere. The only problem then was the grumbling of Dominguez over wishing to stop to play at roulette and other games at the casinos that entertained so many of the aristocrats of Europe once they reached the Italian States. He even protested that the Prince Regent's unwanted wife, Princess Caroline, was quite content to be seen here among the gamesters.

"But not, I think, by your leader, Luther?" Anthony pointed out.

Sir Anthony had watched the gypsy with a hawk's gaze when when he was around Samara, but it was obvious and a great relief for Samara to notice soon enough that whatever motive Dominguez might have in making this trip, sexual interest in his fellow gypsy was not among them. He insisted on handling the reins alone when he took his turn, and Anthony kept Samara beside him night and day, to be sure. Samara was amused, thought not in the least afraid of the dour Dominguez.

She still felt that anything they had to worry about concerning Dominguez was monetary and was relieved when they had gone beyond Marseille and were nearing the town of Nizza, as the Italian States called it. Much of this flowery, warm Riviera shore was already attracting the rest of Europe.

Behind and beyond Nice were the Maritime Alps and the corniches. The roads were steep and difficult, and Anthony became anxious to get his money from the company handling his credit. Surely, his ward and Alexi would have a little trouble between Nice and the Italian States. Even the jewels they possessed would be a mark against them? They would not seem very likely to own them, as they would have to claim. Now, if ever, would be the most likely place to come upon them.

The night before they pulled into the elegant and flower-scented Nice, Dominguez slept on the cot inside the wagon and Anthony and Samara as usual lay in the warm night, on a blanket under the stars, discussing the morrow's plans.

If the town refused to honour Anthony's letters of credit they must tighten their belts and try to reach Genoa through one of the mountainous trails that separated Nice from the Italian seaside area of Lombardy and the Italian States.

"I'll be glad when we have done with Dominguez," Samara murmured suddenly.

Anthony turned his head and look at her, putting one hand over hers. "Not frightened? Not my bold and brave Samara?"

She laughed. "Not as you think of it. But since we left Marseille he has taken more than a little interest in my clothing."

He raised himself up. "What? Has he touched you?"

"There is nothing sensual about it. He often sits watching and jingling coins in the pocket of his jerkin or those wide-legged breeches. He is thinking of money. All the time."

"I imagine so. But when he gets paid it will be entirely the problem of his band whether he steals their shares or not. I can think of better reasons for him to stare at your clothing. Just don't let me catch him."

She could not tell him why Dominguez might be staring at her clothing. She had never told anyone, and only a gypsy would be likely to know, that she hid her 'fortune', all that she had in the world, inside those skirts she wore.

Nice was not a town in which gypsy caravans camped out, as Dominguez reminded Anthony in his surly way, adding, "It is your choice," when nothing was said in reply to his comment.

Samara expected that Sir Anthony did not want to offend her by asking her to look more like one of his race, but she felt reasonably sure neither she nor the gypsy wagon would be a welcome addition in the Riviera town.

She changed to a commonplace black gown with a crimson scarf wide enough to cover much of her bosom. It was less easy to re-dress her hair and finally she tied it back, though the warm breeze ruffled up strands and sooner or later she knew it would look unkempt as usual.

Anthony objected to her attempts to subdue her gypsy look and asked her to wear one of her more obviously gypsy costumes, despite her pointing out that she would be about as welcome as their gypsy wagon in the little Riviera town for much of affluent Europe.

He reminded her, "Sweetheart, I fell in love with a strange, exotic creature. I'm proud of you and what you are. I may as well confess, I prefer your way of life to mine. As far as I am concerned, I never want to go back. I can thank that stupid child, Dilys, for that, at all events."

She didn't believe it, or if he thought it was true, it wouldn't last, but she loved his reassurance and when they drove into town past the growing areas along the beach and esplanade, she sat up proudly beside him as he reached one arm around her lissom waist and murmured, "You must stop believing I am a liar. When I tell you something, I mean it."

"I'm sure you do." She flashed a smile at him, her red lips parting in the sunlight as he leaned over to kiss her.

The wagon rattled into the town, past a park, a square, and on toward what appeared to be a very much more Italianate vicinity, the narrow streets filled with playing children and males in pantaloons and jerkins rather like the Dominguez's. They all stopped to watch as the wagon creaked past them, but the looks the men gave them were not friendly.

Anthony pointed out a two-storey Italian building with many closed shutters against the hot Latin sun and an obscure, badly painted sign reading:

'VETTURI, ROMA.
ASSOC. BEVEL, CONSTANT & LEITHBRIDGE, LONDON.
DECOSTA, PARIS.'

"Bevel, Constant," Sir Anthony announced with satisfaction. "I called on them often in Brussels. We were rather busy, as I recall. Shall we?"

He climbed down and handed the reins over to Dominguez, who hurried to his side. Then Anthony turned to help Samara, but she was standing beside him already. He laughed and shook his head.

Always suspicious, she asked, "Are you going to leave Dominguez with the wagon?"

"What is there to steal? He wants the payment I am about to make him for the band. I'll buy a decent carriage and pair afterward. And we'll be on our way in a matter of hours."

He pinched her nose as if she were a child. "The others know this rogue better than we do. Luther and his people must be confident he will bring it all back. If not . . ."

She agreed after a little thought. "If he kept the money and wagon the word would get about to the other bands, and I wouldn't want to be in his boots, eh, Dominguez?"

The gypsy ignored her and pretended to look

around with interest. Anthony looked at her, smiling but curious. "Are your people really so dangerous?"

"Murder, do you mean? Nothing of that sort. But in our world they die."

"Die? Well, well. I hadn't thought so."

"They die to us. It must be very lonely. No one trusts them or speaks to them. Sooner or later, the *goys* find out and they too honour the silence. They don't trust one who betrays his fellows in any of the Rom."

Anthony looked around, watching the silent movements of Dominguez as he worked on the team.

"You hear that, Dominguez?"

Dominguez grinned without quite smiling. "It is so, señor. You may count upon my loyalty. I would not wish to anger our leader. Luther can be difficult."

The children in the street meanwhile had crowded around the gypsy wagon, trying to peek into the little windows and asking questions about gypsy life.

Anthony offered his arm in his gallant way. Samara hesitated a moment, knowing the sight of her would arouse some interest, not always flattering, but then she accepted and they crossed the street.

The office with its red tiled roof was built for the Mediterranean climate and was less prepossessing than those in some northerly cities. Samara and Anthony entered like two aristocrats and strolled beyond the stuffy shuttered foyer to an office far too heavily furnished for the climate. The two mahogany desks were impressive enough for London and the long shelves crowded with ribbon-tied files took up most of the wall space not devoted to the portrait of an elaborate drawing room in the British Prince Regent's Carlton House.

Obviously, an effort had been made to point out the connection between Vetturi and their London connection with Bevel, Constant and Leithbridge.

A carefully sartorially correct young man at one of the two long desks looked up from a Marseille newspaper and jumped up as he smoothed his brick-red hair. He then saw Samara in her reasonably commonplace gown and pelisse, which offered a drab contrast to her stunning eyes and hair.

The young man cleared his throat and addressed Anthony, who looked reasonably like a travelling Englishman.

"You wished—" he glanced at Samara, "—perhaps a permit for a local performance, signor? A fair? A carnival? I'm afraid that is impossible. At this moment we have a carnival at the foot of one of the corniche roads." He spoke in English with every indication of ordering his visitors out.

Sir Anthony straightened a little. He had never been anything but impressive to Samara and now she was more aware than ever of the arrogance that subdued young Vetturi.

"I fear we are speaking at cross-purposes. I forget my manners." He turned to Samara with respect. "Your Highness, may I present you?"

Taking her cue, she gave him a cool, haughty look out of her forbidding eyes, and said, "You may, Sir Anthony."

Young Vetturi's eyes opened wide and he moved forward.

"I don't understand, signor. Her Highness, you say?"

"The Princess Samara of Parthia," Anthony put in. "Her Highness is being escorted incognito through this area to see the conditions in the Italian States since the end of the wars. The Shah, her distinguished father, may invest, if the Barbary pirates are subdued."

Vetturi fluttered, "Subdued, signor . . . Highness. I can vouch for this area. Below Genoa and towards the Papal States, one cannot say. Sometimes the Papal vessels are not as alert as one would wish. How may I assist you?"

Samara was out of her realm in discussing Sir Anthony's money; so she made a sweeping gesture and said severely, "You must speak to Sir Anthony Linden on the matter. He is, of course, representing my father's affairs to the British Crown. The King trusts him implicitly."

She hoped Anthony admired her performance as much as she did.

She noticed that while Signor Vetturi was bowing and scraping to Anthony, the Englishman gave her a little grin and a faint nod.

Samara then took the high-backed 'Milord' chair that Vetturi offered her obsequiously, but she did not want to hear about Anthony's money and interested herself in the aged volumes and files covering the walls.

If she became involved in Anthony's finances she felt that she would be owned by him, a thought that

227

terrified her. She had always saved every farthing. Since her grandmother's death, she had been completely independent. She did not intend to change now. Fortunately, the coins in her bundle of costumes would keep her free any time she felt she must leave him.

Anthony received his money when the letters of credit, the signatures and personal introductions furnished by Bevel, Constant et cetera had been examined with apologies by Vetturi.

By the time the matter was attended to and Anthony went out of the dusty office with the 'Princess Samara of Parthia' on his arm, Anthony told her, "If our friend Vetturi comes to London, you may be expected to hold a reception for him at the Parthian Embassy."

She laughed. "Is there one? And is there a Shah of Parthia?"

"I doubt it. The last time I heard of the place was in my Roman History studies."

Suddenly, he caught her hand. "Well, I'm damned. Our good-natured mare is back. And our little carriage. What the devil?"

All her suspicions returned.

"And that rogue Dominguez, with the gypsy wagon and team are all gone, you notice."

He was philosophical. "At least all our property seems to be piled under the seat of the carriage. Can you run?"

"Certainly." As if she had not spent her life running over the hills.

They hurried across the road, dodging a carriage, a

team and a big, empty tumbril coming down from the lower corniche.

A tall, dark man strolled around to their side of the carriage and past their mare, who was plaintively protesting, whether at losing the gypsy leader or seeing her previous owners, it was hard to say. There was no sign of Dominguez. The gypsy leader waved to them.

"My friends! You have transacted your business, Dominguez tells me. He asks me to bid you a friend's goodbye. I have work for him to perform. He knows this area better than I do."

Anthony, who had put his hand on the weapon in his pocket, remained smiling.

"You want your money, I take it, and you are kind enough to give us back our equipment—"

"Which we have held in bondage," Luther finished for him. "I asked Dominguez to remove your property from the wagon. Would you be kind enough to glance at the pile of your goods under the seat of your little carriage?"

Anthony took his time in going to examine his worn old portmanteau but Samara was so anxious, she rushed to the bundles and the case beneath the carriage seat. All seemed as it should be. Her bundle of clothing was much as she had left it, the top gown seemingly undisturbed.

Luther watched her, somewhat amused.

"You need not concern yourself, my friend. As I too am trusting Sir Anthony to pay me our fee for the loan of our wagon and team. Was it a fair bargain, Sir Anthony?"

"That remains to be seen. Why are you here? Don't you trust your Dominguez? Or did you change your plans?"

Luther nodded. "Just so. I certainly trust my man, as as much as I trust you, my friend. But my people are now established for the moment at Narbonne and Dominguez would have no way of knowing our plans had changed. I settled my people and came after you."

"Good of you."

"Thank you. I felt it was the least I could do in view of the debt between us."

"Ah!" Anthony said.

"I mean, of course, your little mare and the carriage you had left us as hostage, one might say." He added with his faint smile, "And in the hope of receiving what you owe me."

Anthony laughed and agreed, "Eminently fair." He counted out the British pounds in somewhat soiled paper, with an impressive amount of silver and gold coins in the new, post-Imperial denomination of France, and even some ducats minted by the various Italian States.

Samara thought it was far too much but said nothing. At least they would be on their way in peace.

Again, Luther shook Anthony's hand and pocketed the money he had received. Saluting them both, he patted the mare in a friendly way, and left them in the road. His own horse, a handsome creature which seemed to be an Arab breed, waited nervously for his master. The gypsy leaped on his back with admirable command and waved to Anthony and Samara again as his mount began to gallop up around the turn on the corniche.

Samara rushed to the little carriage, felt a package of crusted bread, some not quite hard fruit and a bottle of red wine, undoubtedly local, or from upper Italy. She thrust the packages down in the bundle among her piles of costumes, above her petticoats with their priceless contents. She saw only the top gown of green satin and black velvet but that, and the tiny gems set in as decor were still safe.

"Thanks be to God!" she murmured to herself. "Shall we be on, Sir Anthony? Your ward and Alexi will have left Genoa any day."

"Right. But we aren't going to follow friend Luther and worthy Dominguez. We've seen the last of them, I devoutly hope."

He leaped up beside her on the little carriage seat and unwound the reins. Then, as she laughed her agreement, he leaned over and kissed her. She returned his kiss, surprised at her own freedom – and by day-light – as he gave the mare the signal to start.

As he had intended, they turned, followed another tumbril of new flowers for sale to the English and Russian royalty now enjoying the difference between this weather and that at home. While Samara looked around at the scene, they swung up onto a high road, avoiding the traffic from the lower corniche into the town.

Samara shared his relief at leaving the Romany caravan and the shifty-eyed Dominguez and spent time admiring the exquisite scenery of the early spring.

After some time, Anthony drew her to him, as though communicating his pleasure in their circumstances to her. When she looked into his eyes and smiled, he said, "No wonder you gypsies are wanderers. It's the only life."

It was so like something she might have expected from another of her people that she felt closer to him than she had ever been.

It was getting on toward sunset when it occurred to him that they hadn't eaten a luncheon, much less breakfast.

"Damn! I should have thought of food in Nice. Can you wait until we reach a town on the border?"

She sat up straight. "Ah! Our Romany friends left us food with my clothes. There must be water for the mare. She hasn't drunk any for the last hour or two."

He stopped the mare under the early spring greenery marking a view of the coastal waters and handed her the reins. Then he got down and retrieved his ancient bag out from under his seat. He opened her bundle of clothing. After a moment he weighed it in his hand, untied it, and took out the bottle of wine and the packages of food. Then he stared at the opened bundle which remained.

"Well, I'm damned! The weight. It's shrunk."

"What!" She looked down over the side.

He weighed it again. "It seemed a little heavier before. Those tiny jewels you wear on the gowns probably . . . No. They are here."

She felt as if she had been stabbed, and threw her body against him, trying to get down from the seat.

She was so panicked he took her by her shoulders and held her against him, his strength preventing her from motion.

"What is it, sweetheart? Look at me. Are you ill?"

"My coins . . . all my money—"

She had never before been so terrified. Her entire life, her freedom and independence, her very soul, was in those coins that had been taken from her petticoats and two of her gowns. Without them, she had no life, as she knew it.

He let her go and reached into the bundle, took out and shook the petticoats, several of them. Then he took her hands and held her.

"Darling, listen to me. There is nothing here, I grant you that. No coins. But it is a small matter to replace them from this sheaf of money I've just gotten. You may believe, I was not such a fool as to pay our friend Luther every shilling. Now, sweetheart, say you love me, kiss me, and we'll set ourselves to decide how quickly we can get on to Genoa and that brat of a ward of mine."

She drew back slowly, forcing a smile. He hadn't the remotest idea of what the coins meant to her. Indeed, he had no real understanding of her at all.

Twenty

S amara made no objection when Anthony lifted her to the seat and followed her up, taking the reins in his palms. He gave the obliging mare a signal and they started off. To Samara's surprise the mare started to turn the cart in the road.

She protested. "You aren't going back!"

He was good-natured about it. "Why not? That gang of gypsies can't travel forever without resting."

"Nor can we. And what of your ward?"

He shrugged. "The devil take the little brat."

"No. Wait. Let me read my cards, at least."

That made him laugh. "You love those coins of yours, but you are willing to trust them to a handful of Tarot cards."

She shook her head. "We can't argue with fate. Give me a few minutes."

She felt that the theft of the coins was a message that she must read correctly. She loved this remarkable companion of hers, but they did not belong together. She knew that when he failed to understand the importance of her tiny, private fortune.

He let the mare move slowly back onto the dusty

road while she reached into her deep pocket and brought out the Tarot deck. He began to watch her, intrigued in spite of himself.

"You haven't a table or a board. How can you read their position, or whatever it is?"

"I'll know."

She laid cards out on her skirts, while he remarked in a friendly but sceptical voice, "Take care. They'll slide together. Will you locate the coins?"

He was right, of course. She was nervous, half convinced she couldn't read any message today, and for the first time in years she wondered if she could get a true reading. No matter.

The Eight of Cups. The only life that she knew was now foreign to her. Was that the message? She felt lost. Hopeless.

Swords. Three of Swords. Painful. A gloomy and dangerous time.

How could she tell? The cards were in no true order and they kept changing because the cart was moving.

Anthony had grown interested. He pointed out: "The Chariot. That should be travel. Good times." He gave her a sidelong glance. "Comrades in happiness."

She looked up, puzzled.

"How did you guess that? Not that it's true. I mean, there is nothing to work with it."

The mare moved abruptly, making room for a tumbril and driver rattling along the road and Anthony put his hand over a falling card.

"There. That's mine."

She moved his hands away and then laughed. He was curious at once.

"Comedy? Good. What does it mean?"

Her dark normal complexion deepened in colour.

"There is much sensuous power shortly. It is the Page of Wands. Happiness in a – a special relationship."

"Ah! I've always been a firm believer in the Tarot."

"Liar!" But she laughed, even though she knew this was one time when the cards had to be wrong. She turned over the next card: The Five of Cups. She shivered.

"Bad?" he asked with surprising sympathy.

"A loss. That's all."

"But not found?"

She nodded.

The mare increased her pace, trotting along.

Neither Samara nor Anthony said anything. He looked as though he might speak but was silent.

She said abruptly, "We've lost time. Never mind the coins. We must get on to Genoa."

They began to make speed. The mare seemed to enjoy the hurry and Samara considered all the Tarot half-truths and contradictions she had read, or perhaps mis-read.

They stopped presently at the top of a rough, jagged cliff, and watered and fed the mare. It was late evening now, going into the night, with the dark waters far below them sparkling in the starlight.

With the mare contented they enjoyed the bread and sausage, the fruit and cheese and the wine. Samara went so far as to jokingly thank Luther and his band of gypsies for the delicious fare. She remarked finally, "I can't believe Luther stole my coins."

Anthony had been thinking over the theft.

"There wasn't time, sweetheart. I expect Dominguez is behind it, cutting the coins off little by little, perhaps while we were driving the team." He thought of her loss that had been swept away.

"I could wring his evil neck."

He laughed but agreed.

Presently, they lay down upon their blanket and made love beneath the top blanket. The night was chill and gave them an even keener delight in discovering the wonders of each other's warm flesh.

They roused themselves before dawn and were on their way down onto the coastal Riviera. There were few signs of the many battles that had currently put the Lombard Kingdom in temporary command of the area.

On the afternoon that they approached the outskirts of of the many-layered seaport of Genoa they were almost sorry to lose their good comrade, the mare and her cart.

However, the second officer, Herbert Cunningham, of British offices of Bevel, Constant and Leithbridge, wanted just such a mare for his mother's carriage, and after a consultation between Anthony and 'Princess Samara' the mare found a comfortable new home.

Anthony, who had intended only to enquire about a young female in the company of an almost equally young gypsy, found his first bit of luck.

A Splash of Rubies

"I wonder if you would favor me about another matter, my dear fellow. You see, Princess Samara's young nephew has run away to Genoa with my very young ward."

"Oh?" Herbert Cunningham's jovial little eyes twinkled, but seeing that this was not the expected mood, he quickly formed a more serious expression. "Too young, I dare say."

"Exactly," Samara told him with the expected air of a princess. "The family would be pleased, but for the children's age. Far too young, both of them. My nephew is the heir to considerable estates and of course, my old friend, Sir Anthony, could not permit his ward's estate to go into her hands until she is eighteen and married, at which time, it will be her husband's property."

"Quite so, signorina – Your – er—" He frowned and looked toward his young clerk for help that was not forthcoming. "Have you reason to suppose they have remained in Genoa?"

Anthony recognised a possible knowledge on his friend's part.

"You know of their problem?"

"Better, my friend. Only a week since, a young English lady, little more than a child, stopped by and spoke with my clerk."

Anthony muttered, "Thank God. Maybe that idiot child is safe at last."

Herbert Cunningham excused himself and crossed the room to his clerk's door.

Anthony looked after them and when Cunningham

had gone out, Samara asked Anthony on an ironic note, "The child is safe?"

He grimaced. "Well, damn it! We can't expect an angelic virgin after all these weeks." He reached across the corner of Cunningham's desk and touched her hand.

"Darling, neither you nor I are virgins at this moment."

She hesitated, amused but trying to see the matter sensibly. "Come now, what's to be done?"

He acted as if his own solution were perfectly correct. "Marry them off as rapidly as possible." He added calmly, "In fact, you and I must marry before we find them. So they won't be shocked by our conduct."

She shook her head at his absurdity and jeered, "Captain Sir Anthony Linden, Justice of the Peace, presents his gypsy bride to His Highness the Prince Royal. I have a delightful view of the scandal it will bring to Brighton. Not to mention his new home in London."

"Rubbish. I've been planning this for weeks."

She was shaking her head at his ridiculous notion when Cunningham returned with a shy-looking youth, obviously uneasy, who gave Sir Anthony a brief look and then stared for several seconds at Samara, both frightened and surprised.

Samara had this effect on some males occasionally and now she merely smiled, hiding her contempt for what she assumed was his cowardice.

Half of her thoughts were still with Anthony and his

naïve belief that they could become a happy, married couple in this modern world of 1817.

"Has this young man seen my nephew and the child?" she asked, ignoring Anthony's friend Mr Cunningham.

The young man cut in quickly, "It was a week gone by, signorina. The pretty little lady wished to sell a piece of jewellery. She had other pieces but the gypsy accompanying—" he avoided Samara and spoke directly to Cunningham, "—the young male, I mean to say – did not think they should sell more than the ear-bob and a ring. The rest would be needed later."

Cunningham interrupted with a dignified apology.

"Naturally, this banking house could do nothing except offer sound parental advice. She was Your Excellency's blood kin, as we assumed from business epistles of Your Excellency's that she carried."

"Then she is still in Genoa," Anthony said with relief.

"I regret, signor, only until yesterday," the clerk reminded them all. "The supercargo of a schooner was in to see Signor Cunningham last evening, shortly after you left for your home. The fellow asked if we could vouch for the young pair. They were boarding his schooner and he wished to know if they were able to pay their passage from Genoa to the Papal States. They wanted to reach Rome. I hope I did right, signor? I said yes."

Cunningham looked surprised but before his English guest he said carelessly, "Quite true."

"When did they leave?" Anthony wanted to know.

The clerk gave his employer an uneasy look. "They should be in port and then Rome very shortly. Unless the Papal Authorities seize all on board as smugglers." Anthony shrugged and grimaced at Samara.

"Well, I seem to recall promising you a Grand Tour of Italy, darling."

Mr Cunningham and his clerk raised their eyebrows but did not make any other reaction to Anthony's endearment.

The banker said on a note of false confidence, "I should think they would be safe. It is true that the judiciary is very strict this time of year in Rome. It is a crime, punishable by death in some cases, to smuggle products that are against the Lenten Laws. However, we have not heard of such punishments these past two years."

"But sir," the clerk cut in anxiously, "will it be safe for – er – wanderers, vagabonds et cetera?"

Gypsies, thought Samara. How careful these people were to avoid mentioning the fate of their Romany victims! Poor Sir Anthony! He was still innocent about such things.

"Yes, yes," Anthony answered impatiently. "But I do know authorities in Rome. We've no time to lose."

"Even so, best go by ship, sir," the young clerk suggested. "There are Papal spies on many of the mail coaches."

"The banking house here sends me to Rome in a few days," Mr Cunningham put in. "On banking affairs, you understand. But it would be a simple thing to investigate your safety. Our banking house does have certain powers in Rome."

Anthony sighed. "Thanks. If we are still in Rome. By that time those brats I am chasing may have taken ship for Spain, or the ports of Africa."

"Dear me, let us hope not."

But it seemed to be the only way out.

While Cunningham and Anthony discussed the kinds of currency, silver, gold and paper, used in many governments of Italy the young clerk, with a running boy of the banking house went down to the busy port and obtained what they called 'the best berthing available' in the night's sailing for the Roman port.

It began to seem especially exciting to Samara, who found this life as colourful as it was unpredictable. While Cunningham was apologising for the crowded conditions at the docks, Anthony saw Samara's eyes sparkling and remarked to her in a low but amused voice, "You love this, don't you?"

Her smile was her answer and he laughed, touching her chin between thumb and forefinger in his habit. "By Gad, I haven't chosen wrong."

The two Englishmen stopped talking long enough to stare at them and then each other.

By the time the clerk returned with the passage arrangements made, Anthony and Samara were ready with their bundles and bags and Mr Cunningham remarked in admiration, "If I were young again, Sir Anthony, I would envy you these adventures you appear to be having."

"Yes. And enjoyed every minute of it," Anthony

243

boasted, taking Samara's hand. He saw her smile and added, "That is to say, almost every minute. I didn't like limping along for a week or so."

Cunningham walked to the door with them.

"You seem perfectly sound now, sir, if I may say so. I hope to see you and your ward safe and sound in Rome very soon." A little late he remembered Samara, "And Your Highness, of course. A splendid companion."

"All of that," Anthony called back as they emerged into the shadowy hall and were on their way.

The company's young runner was waiting for them in the busy street and they found themselves in what, to Samara, was a fascinating *mélange* of alleys, bound through a mysterious maze that ultimately must lead to the wharves. All of the Mediterranean did business in the great mercantile port and Samara did not know which way to look in order to see everything that was exciting and strange.

She tried not to think this great adventure would end shortly and see her back on Heaton Clough, or among the busy gypsies in Dorset. As her companion locked her arm in his protectively, she wondered if she would ever let herself see him again when they returned to England.

Surely, she had never needed anyone; yet he was behaving now as if he were a part of her life for ever. A ridiculous dream, totally impossible to make real.

Twenty-One

I t did occur to Samara once or twice that she had found seasickness unpleasant, but there would be great excitement in sailing out of the grand, unbelievably active harbour of Genoa where sailing ships from much of the Mediterranean Europe moved majestically in and out every day.

She hadn't guessed either that the way to the harbour meant passing down many steps, along the intricate alleyways, past sellers of strange, odd-smelling seafood. There were deepwater fish and dangerous-looking shellfish crawling about on wet counters, waiting to be picked up, their claws avoided.

She wanted to stop and purchase some to save them from the boiling pot. Something of her feeling must have caught Anthony's attention because he saw the glow in her eyes at the thought of this adventure, and she looked up defiantly.

"Are you shocked that human beings sometimes think themselves part of that strange other-world?"

He shook his head. "I often think that myself. I must confess, though, I also eat them. I'm sorry."

She laughed and tightened her fingers around his

arm. "Not at all. Your God and mine would probably find it very wasteful in just letting them grow old and die."

"You're probably right, sweetheart." He turned to the left with her, down another alley and set of steps toward the ships at anchor in the near distance.

He said unexpectedly, "I sometimes think I never knew what it was to enjoy companionship until I met you at that horse fair."

She dismissed this with a pleased grin. "Rubbish. There was always the Lady Elaine."

"And there always will be, in some poor devil's life, but not in mine. What a damned bore she is!"

She could only be pleased with that, whether he exaggerated or not.

The running boy from Mr Cunningham's office had been hurrying along ahead of them and as they descended to the open wharves, the ship's chandlers', and numerous taverns, Anthony was pleased.

"The boy is pointing to that schooner at anchor in the harbour ahead of us. Not very impressive but it should serve."

"It looks bigger than the little Spanish ship looked." Was that good or bad, she wondered. "I devoutly hope it doesn't rock about," she remarked, rolling her dark eyes heavenward.

He laughed and assured her on very little authority that it looked as though it had a steady bottom.

A considerable cargo was being loaded, which made Anthony say, "I trust that is not all contraband."

There was so much cargo being loaded that Samara

and Anthony found themselves jammed into a dory with barely enough room for their few possessions. This did not matter to Anthony, and even less to Samara, who remembered all too vividly the loss of her worldly estate.

Reaching the schooner's side as the ship rode a little roughly on the blue Ligurian waters, Anthony took the rope ladder with his usual agility. Samara scrambled up the splintering wooden hull, cheered by two sailors who lifted her to the deck before the surprised and admiring Anthony could do so.

They were shown to a tiny cabin. Anthony paid the first mate for the use of the dark hole, which looked reasonably comfortable to Samara, although he frowned at it when they were alone.

"Sweetheart, it's a bit of luck that I didn't promise you the moon and stars on this famous Grand Tour."

She was looking around and found it perfectly adequate, although the bunks were nothing but two hammocks and the furnishings were a three-legged stool and an ancient deal table marked with what appeared to be knife cuts. Evidently, it had been used formerly in a butcher's shop.

"Very easy," she said.

He laughed and hugged her to him, remarking, "You make me feel that this is our bridal night."

She shook her head but suddenly, on an impulse, turned her head a little and touched his hand, on her shoulder, with her lips. Obviously pleased, he raised her chin and covered her lips with his.

Seconds later, a step in the passage made him raise

his head. He looked out the partially open door and then, to her surprise, muttered, "Good God!" and quickly drew her back further into the cabin, slamming the door with his foot.

Puzzled, she asked, "What is it?"

He dismissed it too lightly. "No one. Another passenger."

From his reaction it didn't sound quite so simple. She broke away and started to the closed door, anxious and wondering.

He reached for her hand, holding her back.

"Don't. It is an old friend of ours."

"Friend?" For some reason she thought at once of Lady Elaine and wondered what the woman was doing on a schooner in the Ligurian sea.

He reached again for her hand but then thought better of it.

"The fellow seems to have been thrown out of the band. Not surprising. Probably they caught him stealing from them."

"Not—!" She threw the door open just as a rattling sound shook her back into his arms.

"The noise is the anchor. Our fellow passenger is Dominguez. Too late now. We'll have to live with him for the next day or so. Then I'll get the authorities in Rome on his trail."

Dominguez? Did he still have her entire life's savings? She guessed what might happen. Quite probably, Dominguez would be made to give up the amount he had stolen, if Anthony had as much power in Italy as his banking houses seemed to indicate. But it would not be in the coins, many of them gold, that she had hoarded for her future.

It would be meaningless if they gave her paper or foreign currency from countries currently at war or usually bankrupt. Very much like Anthony's offer to replace her coins with money which would not be the same at all. She had never trusted anyone with her coins. Not even Anthony. He had never understood that. He thought all money was the same.

She said finally, "Well, if he is here now, we can't very well throw him overboard. Besides," she gave him a grin that seemed to surrender, "we may persuade him to give up my coins."

He pinched her cheek but confessed, "I doubt even you could do that. Leave the matter to me. There are ways."

"There are. I agree."

He looked at her suspiciously but she returned his look with such innocent assurance he could not argue with her, whatever he thought privately about her intentions toward Dominguez.

His thoughts were obviously still on Samara's possible trouble with the gypsy and as she untied her bundle of clothing, he asked her casually, "Have you often had difficulties, living alone? It's exceedingly rare."

She knew he must be enquiring about other men, other loves.

"Especially for a gypsy?"

"Well, yes. They usually travel together."

She shook out the green and black gown vigorously.

249

Anthony sneezed and waited for her answer. She said carelessly, "You mean, why do I carry a weapon? Merely a precaution, since my grandmother died."

"But you were a child when she died?"

"I didn't want any other company. I had friends when I was lonely. Marika and Stefan and their band."

"All those years you have lived alone?"

She look at at him. "Of course. I certainly wouldn't live with the men who – who – Never mind."

He reached for her hand and squeezed it. "But not now."

She repeated, "Not now," but her emphasis on the last word was evident. He must have noticed. She added honestly, "I didn't know you then."

"Thank you." He kissed the palm of her hand and she felt the excitement that he always stirred in her since the first time she met and would not admit his attraction, even to herself.

She continued smoothing out the velvet skirt while he laughed and then took out a razor and little shaving mirror from his valise. He had shaved this morning but seemed to feel this scene required a note of domesticity which she found oddly exciting also.

The schooner had already gotten under way and they could hear the usual shouts, cries and orders overhead. The night glow of light, torches and lamps around the harbour through the porthole began to fade as the old vessel passed the Genovese port and the shoreline beyond.

By the time the ship was sailing into the main channels of the busy Ligurian sea, and Samara had taken a brisk bath with a sponge and a small pail of salt water, Anthony returned from the passage and his questioning about meals, if any.

She had put on a clean shift and two petticoats, and Anthony stood in the doorway a moment, enjoying the spectacle her dark golden flesh made for him, barely covered by her shift and petticoats.

He closed the door behind him and shot the bolt, explaining as he looked at her, "I don't want to be selfish, but those seagoing disasters out there don't deserve this view of you."

She grinned and took up the green and black gown.

"Does that mean we are to have something in the nature of supper? Or even dinner?"

"None other." He crossed the room to begin buttoning her gown, suggesting to her, "You see how very obliging I could be as a husband?"

She was too anxious about getting her coins back from Dominguez to react as she should, but she managed to laugh lightly.

"Is the captain a friend of our Dominguez?"

"I doubt it. I suspect Dominguez has sold him some information. Probably about the timing of the Papal luggers on patrol. That is, if we are actually carrying contraband."

He was watching her. He reminded her gently, "Isn't it better to permit the return of the coins legally?"

"If I were a Gentile, perhaps. But you and I both know the authorities of most countries would not believe me."

He pulled a lock of her already dishevelled hair.

"I hate to boast, darling, but you do have me. And I am generally trusted."

He paused, then said quietly, but in a firm tone she recognised, "Remember one thing. Don't under any circumstances, mention your coins. If one of us must, I'll do it."

Surprised, she stared at him.

"Why not?"

"Because I want the matter handled legally. The coins must be recognised as yours. Legally. If you do this my way, we may succeed. Agreed?"

She might accept everyone's word and signature, like the good legal counsel he himself was. But she remembered too well the gypsy prisoners in the cart on their way to a terrible fate. As a Justice of the Peace, Sir Anthony had taken someone's word for their guilt.

She, on the other hand, like many of her people, did not take another's word if it involved her. She did not agree with Anthony, and thought his conclusion naïve, but she did not want to lie directly, so she shrugged and smiled in what appeared to be an assurance. She would not press the captain on the matter, though later, if she found any way of uncovering the truth, she would do so.

Since he could not read her mind, they went out happily into the passage. She swayed with the tidal changes of the old ship, and had to admit the strength of his arm, when she would have crushed her own arm against an open door, was more than welcome.

She admitted to herself, as she had done several times before on their journey, that in almost every way,

Sir Anthony was the companion she might have dreamed of, if she had known he existed. It was probably too late now. But one could still dream. The open door revealed a tiny cabin practically filled by a bunk, a porthole, a table with a ladder-backed chair and three stools. The stools were for guests or the two mates. The captain surprised Samara by his heavy, tough-bodied appearance and strong features. He was probably somewhat over forty, but there was no mistaking his iron fists and the hard look in his small, unexpectedly blue eyes.

He got up, gave Sir Anthony a more or less respectful nod with just the hint of a bow, and was waving Samara to one of the stools when he got a clear look at her by the swinging lamp overhead. He opened his eyes wider and said with a politeness that did not fit his piratical looks, "Honoured, signorina. My English, not good, no. But my pleasure of your company, very much, *si.*" He looked over at Anthony. "You might make me prepared, signor. Not often passengers like the signorina."

Anthony was amused, but rising to the occasion, he said, "Princess Samara di Parthia, Captain Cordona." He added, "The Principessa is on her way to bring home her nephew, a boy who ran away with my ward. A childish business, but I suppose love will find a way."

The captain grunted what sounded like a negative and began to break his bread into pieces. There seemed to be no hard tack on this ship. He looked up at Samara every minute or so when he wasn't taking mouthfuls of food or eyeing the starved-looking cabin boy who hurried in and out, evidently hoping not to be seen.

Samara was anxious to know what the captain would say about Dominguez and was grateful to Anthony, who casually brought up the subject.

"I seemed to recognise one of the – was it passengers? – as we came aboard. Very dark. A gypsy, I imagine."

Always sensitive to the difference everywhere accepted between Gentiles and Romany, Samara raised her head.

The captain nodded. "*Ah, si.* Called by name Dominguez. A fellow of mystery. My men tell me he hints of his gold. We are to drop him at Naples. I ask myself, where does he go with this gold?"

Anthony caught Samara's eye but she did not answer his look. He agreed with the captain's question. "He is the same who stole gold from the Principessa in Marseilles. We hope to have it returned."

"I intend to see that it is returned," she cut in sharply.

The captain looked at her, surprised as much by the look in her black eyes as by her words. He grinned. "The Principessa feels her wrongs like a Corsican. I myself must doubt that the gold is here, but it is for us to wish the Principessa well." He examined his bread for weevils, pounded and shook them out, and remarked. "But it would be well to take care. The Papal Fleet is small at the moment, no bigger than a few luggers, but hard. I have seen with these eyes the axe that takes the heads off thieves and murderers. Especially in Lent. At a square in Rome. One pays to see the sight."

But Anthony said, "Doubtless, they deserved it."

"But these were accused of theft."

The captain's words seemed almost like a deliberate reminder to Anthony, who did not like the subject and changed it rapidly.

"Let us hope justice prevails all around."

"As you say, signor. I drink to justice." The captain raised his rum mug in a toast and then nearly buried his face in the mug as he drank.

To Samara, one thing had been learned at this macaroni and fish dinner with the captain. She suspected Dominguez still held her coins. If they didn't get the coins back before they left the ship in the Tyrennian Sea and took the road inland to Rome, they would probably never see them again.

After they had bid goodnight to Captain Cordona, Samara saw her companion was reasonably satisfied, which was not her mood at all.

She began by hinting mildly, "Isn't it possible to examine his room, or hammock; wherever Dominguez sleeps?"

"He probably has them on him," Anthony pointed out. "Granted that the captain seems interested in keeping us away from the coins, it may even be that Dominguez really doesn't have them."

"Do you believe that?"

"Frankly – no."

They both laughed.

In the harsh voice that sometimes startled strangers, she said then, "We might strip him naked and shake the coins out of him. Dominguez, I mean."

"My dear child, I am shocked. Utterly shocked."

They both grinned at the sinister picture she had summoned up.

They went along the narrow passage, swaying rhythmically as the schooner cut through what briefly proved to be calm seas, and Samara studied a couple of doors, wondering if Dominguez could be sleeping in the foc'sle with the rest of the crew not on watch.

As Anthony opened their own door, she looked back at a cabin crowded beneath the deck ladder. He had let her hand go but stepped back now to see what delayed her. She said, "It's ajar."

"No."

"But it is." She pushed the door open and looked into the tiny cabin. It was more austere than the captain's cabin or their own, but very likely used for an occasional passenger.

Anthony came back to join her and put his arm out, waiting for her to take it.

She hesitated, looked around the little cubicle. The jerkin Dominguez had worn when travelling with them was bundled up on the cot. Samara's fingers itched to examine it but Anthony gave her arm a slight tug and she decided to wait.

They returned to the cabin assigned to them, she piqued and Anthony amused at this but also obviously determined to have his own way. She found herself in two minds about his insistence that she obey him. She was annoyed but she found his authority with her also to her liking. She certainly did not admire weakness. Besides, as she admitted to herself, there were times when he actually knew more than she about life.

"Suppose the coins are in that jerkin," she suggested as he closed their cabin, shutting out the world of sea and sky.

"Then they will be there when we dock," he reminded her. "I doubt if the fellow does much swimming. Come to bed, darling. Don't keep me in suspense."

How domestic it sounded! She found it not unattractive. She thrilled inwardly to the knowledge that he wanted her, and she could hardly doubt that. Their moments in bed together showed her the life that she had been missing. When they were in the narrow bunk, laughing at how crowded they were, the fact only made them appreciate each other more.

Still, there were minutes during the night when her thoughts returned anxiously to the rat-like Dominguez and that jerkin with several pockets. She wondered if she would ever get her fingers on those coins. It was a matter of pride and of principle. It was the rock of freedom on which her life had been built since she had looked around as a child and found no one there.

But she could not see how Sir Anthony, a man with a five-hundred-year pedigree, could understand the importance to her of some gold coins.

She was awakened very early the next day by scuffling, jeers and laughter in the passage from several sailors going off-duty. They appeared to be arguing in a friendly way about treasures, but there was no definite indication that they might know about her coins.

Then there was Dominguez's voice: "I told you, it was merely a boast. And too much rum."

Had he been boasting about her coins to the others? There was no way of knowing yet.

Later, Anthony mentioned Dominguez's 'treasure' to the captain but Cordona only laughed.

"They all have treasures, signor. It is the standard discussion. All lies."

"I can swear before the Papal authorities that the coins belong to the Principessa," Anthony said.

The captain waved his hand. "As you say, sir." He added with a heavy-lipped smile, "If we are not both wrong."

Anthony started to say something, then changed his mind. "You are right, Captain. If her coins were stolen and not lost, as I suspect, they are probably in Constantinople by now."

The captain considered this happily. "It is very possible, signor. It was perhaps all an absurdity."

Samara gasped and then understood. The captain had decided that if Dominguez carried some expensive coins there was no reason to divide them with Anthony and his 'principessa'.

In the passage Samara and Anthony looked at each other. He shook his head regretfully.

"It would seem you were right. That old pirate has found the coins are here and intends to get them himself."

It was sickening but they weren't through yet. If Sir Anthony's law-abiding methods failed, she would rely upon other methods with which she was familiar.

Meanwhile, Dominguez must know they were aboard because he had kept out of their way so carefully.

Anthony excused himself to discuss what First Mate Mateo knew of the magnificent, still-powerful city of Rome, explaining the problem of finding Miss Dilys Linden.

There was a great deal of noise shifting cargoes during the rest of the day as the schooner crossed through the Tyrennian Sea, with its load to be transported overland to Rome and the rest readied for the Kingdom of the Two Sicilies.

Once the thieving Dominguez was near a large port, Samara knew there would be little chance of retrieving her precious coins. She had thought this should matter more than any other event, even the finding of Anthony's ward, but it occurred to her on their last night before the docking for Rome that the minute they found Dilys Linden, there would be nothing more to keep her and Anthony as companions and lovers that they had been on their long journey.

She had been so sure that they were not destined to remain together but as the time of separation grew closer, she dreaded it. Yet, she still knew there could be no other solution. She found herself thinking of this even more than the recovery of her coins.

Early the following morning, as they passed through the busy waterway crowded with vessels readying to offload for Rome and the Papal States, Captain Cordona met them on deck and pointed out a small lugger crowded with several uniformed officers of the local navy. It was headed out from shore toward a battered ship with strange latten sails, which the captain, with his spyglass at his eye, guessed was bound for Messina.

"Well then, my friends, I know that so-innocent ship. It trades in slaves. They are captured from our own Christian ships. I would avoid them in any waters beyond Messina."

"Will the Papal authorities arrest them?" Samara asked. She was not really afraid of the ship in these waters, but after all, she was not one of the Christians on board Captain Cordona's ship who knew the authorities would save her.

Captain Cordona laughed and Anthony told her, "Not my companion. Unless you've committed a capital crime." He added jokingly, "You haven't, have you?"

The captain lowered his glass.

"You might like to have your luggage at hand, Principessa. It will be easier to see that you are early off, so one hopes. As for the signor, there is but his case, isn't that so?"

"Quite so. What of the other passenger? Is our friend Dominguez packing to disembark?"

The captain shook his head. "Not until the Two Sicilies."

"And his treasure goes with him?"

As Anthony spoke, he glanced out at the Papal

lugger which was pulling away from the Messina-bound ship.

Captain Cordona suggested, "The police, they are for us next, signor. It is as well if you are here with your passport papers. To introduce yourself and the Principessa."

"Yes. We will see to everything," Anthony called back to the captain as he and Samara went down to the lower passage. Samara glanced over at the little cabin in the lower passage and heard some bustling around inside and a case of some kind dragged across the cabin deck.

Anthony was asking her something about her bundle of clothing, mentioning that he should have thought to get her a valise in Genoa and did not hear the muffled sounds in Dominguez's cabin.

She said nothing and went on with Anthony to to their own cabin.

He was ready in seconds, picked up his own valise and the bundle of her costumes.

"Ready?"

She nodded and they were going up the companion-ladder again when she caught her breath and cried, "Go on and see the police. I just remembered. I left my nightrail when I dressed this morning."

He smiled, showing an understanding of women's furbelows and was about to turn back but she looked out on deck.

"I see the men in uniform. I hope you can explain to them about Dominguez."

He hesitated, then touched her hand and went up on

deck. She hurried back down and quietly pushed open Dominguez's little cabin door. He did not hear her at first. He was busy doing something to the bottom of a gentleman's valise, worn but thickly built. It seemed obvious to her that he was carefully cutting away the inner layer at the bottom of the bag. It required heavy material and he had one hand wrapped in a 'palm', a piece of canvas used by carpenters on board ship. In the other hand was a large, strong carpenter's needle.

As he edged the coins under the false bottom of the case, she watched him. For two or three minutes he worked, then some sound, the creak of the ship, or even her breathing, made him aware that he was being watched. He looked up with a grin, partly of fright and partly of toothy fury.

"The gypsy devil!"

"Give them to me. All I have to do is cry out."

He was recovering rapidly.

"In my cabin, you bitch! I mentioned these. Everyone knows they are mine."

He had dropped the canvas 'palm' and raised the long, strong needle. She backed away instinctively with one hand behind her, reaching into her sash. His reaction only made her as furious as he was. Her fingers searched for the knife but it was missing. It must have fallen out of the sash. He got to his feet, the lengthy steel needle still in his hand, and made a lunge at her with it. She eluded him, demanding, "Drop them."

"All I must do is say you robbed me! Who will believe you?"

He lunged again, barely missing her, and she swung around, kicking at his groin with her sandalled foot. He screamed.

She thought for an instant that she had won, and reached down to pick up the coins with their bits of glued thread torn away from their obverse sides.

Before she could stand up something in the doorway behind her struck the back of her head and she went down, falling at Dominguez's feet.

After that, for a minute or two there were sounds of scuffling, another piercing screech that ended in a gurgle, and Dominguez fell across her body. Then there were running feet, past her into the passage. Someone else was hurrying down the companion-ladder.

She stirred, regained her senses, belatedly remembering where she was, and felt herself lifted up and dragged away from under Dominguez's body. She was being lifted into Anthony's arms in spite of her struggles.

"It's over now, darling. Take a deep breath. And don't talk!"

She tried to look around her. They were not alone. Dominguez lay crumpled on the deck unmoving, but two handsome young Italians in uniform had crowded into the little cabin and were puzzling out the scene.

"A quarrel between two gypsies over some coins," one of them insisted. "But could she strangle him?"

"Someone did," the other officer said as he examined the dead man's throat with its coagulated blood and spittal.

From Anthony's arms she stared at the crowded cabin, her vision momentarily blurred and her head aching. She complained, "Someone else came into the cabin. He hit me on the head."

Captain Cordona interrupted. "It is so simple, no? This Englishman he was with me and heard the gypsy female cry out. He left me, came down at once and saw the money on the floor. Either he or the female stabbed our passenger Dominguez."

"But why?" the officer asked. "To defend the woman?"

The captain rubbed his jaw.

"The Englishman had told me this Dominguez stole money from him. Perhaps the woman tried to get it back. You see the coins that fell from her when the English gentleman took her up in his arms."

"No. He knew nothing!" Samara cried angrily.

"Be quiet!" Anthony ordered her, but she finished.

"They were my coins. I wanted them back before he left the ship. But I didn't stab him."

Anthony said, "She is delirious. I want to speak to the Papal Legate in Rome."

The two officers looked at each other. One of them said, "In due time, signor. Meanwhile, you and the gypsy woman must join yesterday's haul. It is the law. We have both theft and murder to deal with."

"Come along," the other police officer ordered. "As for you, Captain Cordona, you will make your declaration. Maybe also, Captain, a deposition about your crew. The gypsy woman was rendered unconscious by someone. Some weapon."

A Splash of Rubies

In spite of Anthony's arm, tightly around her shoulders, she went on, "There had to be another man come in while I argued with Dominguez. I was struck on the back of the head."

"That may have been this gentleman who calls himself Anthony Linden."

"What else is possible?" put in Captain Cordona. "I saw him go below decks myself."

The two police nodded to each other. "Very likely to assist the woman in getting back the coins."

Anthony sighed as if bored by their stupidity.

"Very well. I will go with my betrothed—" That raised their eyebrows. "—and make our statements before competent authorities."

This was a mistake.

"I assure you, signor," said one of the officers, "we are competent authorities. Come! The male will be separated from the female so that there may be no plotting together."

Anthony raised his voice. "Now, look here! I am who I say I am and I am affianced to this lady."

Samara insisted at the same time, "He had nothing to do with it. He arrived after I was struck. He saved me."

It was useless. They paid no attention and relied on the lying captain, hoping to find the coins, no doubt, although two of them were still on the deck of the cabin.

She knew she had been wrong in trying to claim her coins, one of the few times in her life she had understood this, but to make Anthony suffer was the outside of enough.

Only Anthony's low voice in her ear and his hand warmly on her arm kept her from more useless protests.

"Darling, think of it as an adventure. As soon as I can speak to the authorities, it will be all right."

She turned in his arms and clung to him. She wanted to keep saying, "I'm so sorry. It was my fault. I should have listened," but he shook his head and she didn't get all the words out.

Then they were separated and she could hardly believe what she saw when his wrists were tied behind him and he was led up the ship's ladder before her. They were bound for separate longboats.

Twenty-Two

T here were moments when, usually as a child, Samara had been hustled around, pushed and shoved very much as she was today, across the deck and down over the side, having herself painfully dropped the last few feet into the longboat bobbing in the waters below.

But in those long gone days she had not met Sir Anthony Linden. She had thought all gypsies might be treated this way if they couldn't protect themselves. She hadn't known what it was to lose a lover and bosom companion like Anthony.

Now, she wondered if she would ever see him again.

Her wrists were tied behind her, her skirts ripped and torn in the departure from Captain Cordona's schooner, but nothing mattered except Anthony in the other boat which had already started for the shore, propelled by the oarsmen of the Papal police.

In spite of all that had happened, she managed to get to her feet painfully and answer his nod to her from the other boat. He almost seemed to smile. Somehow, at this moment, it meant more to her than a world of coins, gold or silver.

One of the oarsmen stuck his bare foot out to trip her back into place between the police and she was surprised when one of the police reached out and slapped him with one neatly gloved hand.

So these officers were at least as polite as the Riding Officers who had arrested her that day in England. How long ago it seemed!

She looked at the Italian officer and murmured in English, "Thank you."

He did not smile but he blushed and looked away almost shyly.

The waters were surprisingly calm this early morning and no one was seasick, but she was more interested in trying to make out the boat that contained Sir Anthony and the unfettered Captain Cordona, although the latter seemed to be under guard as well.

All communications between the two boats ended at the dock where the men were to be sent on their way in a tumbril apparently headed for Rome.

One of the officers remained with Samara while the shy one went across the sandy, rocky beach to a solid-looking building with a broken tile roof. This housed the other prisoners taken from ships seized in the last few days.

Samara hoped against hope that she would get one last glimpse of Anthony as he was pushed up into the tumbril, but while she was waiting under guard in the sandy shore she saw a surly prisoner brought out of the the building with the tile roof. His arms, lashed behind him at the elbows, were then roped loosely to Anthony's wrists and the two men were joined to a scrawny, frightened-looking youth of about eighteen or twenty. Samara tried to catch Anthony's eye but three new prisoners, all women, were herded out of the same house and joined Samara, forming a barrier against her view of Anthony.

Samara was stupified by everything that had happened in the last hour. Her head ached from the blow she had received in Dominguez's cabin. Once Anthony was out of sight, she made no objection to being lifted into the tumbril for the women.

This second tumbril moved off in the dusty track of the first, while the officers and uniformed guard, bulky and bored with the entire affair, permitted the females to squat on straw in the tumbril.

One of the females, a slip of a girl, sat there with her head buried in her hands and her light, wispy hair fluttering around her piquant face. The girl gave a great sigh and looked up to stare around at the scene.

Samara winced and touched the back of her head gingerly, but the young girl, staring around vacantly, looked familiar to her in spite of her unkempt look and filthy clothing. Samara frowned, but the headache remained, and she closed her eyes.

With the patient, bored assistance of the two oxen, the tumbril rattled off toward Rome, wandering in the general direction taken by the muddy, green Tiber River. Samara, seated with her back to the afternoon light, hoped her headache would gradually disappear before they reached Rome. She needed all her senses to discover how she might escape this trap and still help

Anthony in this ridiculous charge of murder. It was many years since she had paid heed to anyone but herself and she was surprised that she found it far more nervewracking to be frantic about the safety of the only person in the world whom she loved.

There was much activity around the tumbril, with horsemen galloping past private carriages drawn by splendid teams, and aged diligences pulled by dray horses, filled with dozens of people of the countryside, with their chickens, ducks and buckets of eels and fish.

During the minutes when she had her eyes open, Samara thought the whole world was either heading into or out of the great centre of Christianity. Small wonder they were indifferent or cruel to her people, Samara thought. They had their own glorious world. They could afford their arrogance.

She closed her eyes again, grateful that her headache was beginning to die away, when a soft hand reached out, touched the stream of her black hair and a young voice exclaimed in English with astonishment, "It's you! Wake up, Samara. Do wake up. I need you."

Dilys Linden! Of course, she would need someone, and Samara was closest at hand.

Samara opened her eyes. Dilys would have shaken her but she took the girl's hands and easily forced them away. She looked the girl over.

"It seems we meet at last. Where is Alexi?"

Dilys giggled. "What a dear! He's in such trouble. You must save him. We were on a ship that carried countraband and when they searched us they found the ruby set in Alexi's jacket. Without thinking, I told

270

them poor Alexi was abducting me, and they wanted to execute him and let me go. But what would I do alone? So I changed my story and said it was a harmless jest." She added resentfully, "So they took me prisoner, saying I must have stolen Cousin Anthony's jewels."

"To be precise," Samara reminded her, "that actually is your crime."

Dilys dismissed this with a quick wave of the hand. "Oh, don't joke. I must get out of this awful country. They've been abominable to me. Cousin Anthony would never let them treat me so horridly if he knew."

Around them in the tumbril other females watched in various stages of boredom. None of them apparently understood English.

Looking over the girl, who had recovered her normal self-possession, Samara realised this was all one could expect of her.

"Where is Alexi now?"

Dilys shrugged. "They took him ahead yesterday for questioning, poor dear! Cousin Anthony will have to save him. There is no one else, you know. These people don't even speak a normal language."

"What a pity." Samara waited briefly, hoping the girl would show just a smidgin of concern, if not about Alexi and Anthony, at least about her own future. Such was not Dilys's problem, however. Obviously, she had enough to concern her in the subject of Dilys Linden. Considering the rude awakening the girl might receive in time to come, Samara could almost pity her.

There was a stirring around them and Samara

noticed that the women seemed to be readying themselves to get up and climb down from the tumbril.

She looked up, saw what appeared to be a forest of towers, castles, temples, religious edifices, and the busy River Tiber. The tumbril was rattling across one of these bridges and the women around her were pointing out magnificent old towers and lingering longest over a huge dome crowning a religious building across the Tiber.

Dilys also pointed it out. "Look, Samara! That's St Peter's. Isn't it splendid?"

Samara thought it was more impressive than much of London but spent little time over it. Somewhere in the Renaissance splendour of the great city was Anthony Linden. Would she ever see him again?

She had expected to be taken to one of the towering castles or to an old building like Newgate whose purpose was all too evident. Instead, the oxen plodded on, keeping near the river, and made their way, undisturbed, toward a grand and imposing square filled with a shifting, pushing crowd, heading as near the centre of the square as possible.

A fountain marked the centre of the square but at this minute it was dry and the only water it contained was in the very bottom of its big stone saucer. Some madcaps, mostly young, had their dirty hands in the basin scooping up water, throwing it on the crowd, to the fury and yells of those waiting for some entertainment on a platform and a flight of stairs just beyond the fountain.

There was no getting through the crowd and the

oxen balked, finally settling where they were, surrounded tightly by the mob.

"Why are we waiting?" Dilys whispered. "What is it?"

Samara began to suspect and pulled the girl away from the splintered edge of the tumbril. Even young Dilys didn't deserve that horror.

And horror it was!

Two men in black, with tight pantaloons and jerkins that looked like Pierrot costumes came stalking through the crowd. Then another came behind them. He carried a long-handled axe and the other men appeared to be his attendants. They walked up the steps. One of the attendants put a black mask over the executioner's head and eyes. He turned away from them and for an instant, looked out over the crowd like an actor, supervising the attendance for his performance. Samara fancied his eyes glittered through the mask. Then he looked down the steps. Two priests appeared through the crowd as escorts to the condemned, a sullen, brutish-looking man thirty to forty years old boldly looking around at his audience.

An officer in the tumbril muttered something to his fellow officer, then said in English to Samara: "A Barbary pirate. He deserves it."

Nevertheless, Samara turned her head away, swallowing hard. Dilys hadn't turned quickly enough and was caught staring, open-mouthed, as the big pirate's legs were kicked by the two assistants and his knees gave away. He found himself kneeling at the block.

Everything was over very quickly, a shriek, and a deafening yell from the crowd.

Samara did not look back but still the sounds were audible. Several boys came yelling and pushing through the crowd, waving red kerchiefs that spilled drops on the thrusting mob. Others in the mob tried to break away. But unlike Samara, they were all chattering over how successfully the criminal had died.

When Samara looked back, wondering if Dilys needed comforting, the girl looked faint and pale but her eyes were wide and she did ask, "Is it over?" Other prisoners in the crowd giggled and pointed young Dilys out to the other prisoners.

The officers had called out to the carters several times and the old man finally got the oxen on their way through the crowd, past a huge, circular building under a great Roman dome. From here the tumbril found its way until it stopped at a low, narrow stone building that looked as though the top stories, or perhaps the upper walls, had been removed.

By the time the women were being piled out of the tumbril, Samara had gotten Dilys on her feet and the girl, though still pale, managed to boast, "They won't believe me in London or Brighton. I actually saw an execution." She looked up at Samara, her big eyes suddenly worried. "You don't think they will do something like that to us?"

"Certainly not. Have you no confidence in your cousin?"

She wished she herself might believe it. Could she bear to know that Sir Anthony had died like the Barbary pirate?

She and Dilys were the last to be taken in through

the iron-barred gates so narrow the Papal police had to enter sideways. The building had not yet been repaired after one of the late brawls at the time of Waterloo in Belgium, and Samara couldn't imagine what she and Dilys would find within.

There was nothing on the ground floor except a high-roofed hall with a view of the Tiber on the far side opposite the entrance and a guard leaning one foot on an historic cerule chair and drinking a Neapolitan wine. He set his glass on the chair and came to attention when he sighted the Papal guards.

Samara and Dilys were the last of the five women whom the guards beckoned down the steps at the back of the hall. These steps were wet and slippery and Dilys complained to Samara, "They don't know who I am. They don't know Cousin Anthony was far more important in the war than these silly Italians."

Samara glanced around, saw the guard beating a truncheon against his hip, and nudged Dilys. The girl had sense enough to understand and keep quiet, though she muttered something to herself.

As they reached the bottom of the steps, they were both shoved toward a narrow cell of some kind, with a lamp swinging from the rough, plastered ceiling.

The other women had already been pushed into the cell and as Samara, expecting the worst, started after them, she was stopped with Dilys. The officer at the top of the steps called down, "Hold those two. They are to be interrogated."

One of the women being hustled into the cell called

to Samara, her voice like a rooster's cackle, and kept laughing.

Samara went back up the steps with Dilys clutching at her skirts.

"What is it?" Samara asked. "Why are we separated from the others?"

At the top of the steps the young Papal officer had been arguing with the guard and now explained to Samara in English, "There was an escape in the street a short while ago. You are to be interrogated with the prisoner when his partner is brought in."

Dilys, clutching Samara, had begun to shiver but whispered, "Maybe Alexi escaped. Oh, thank God! I knew he would save me."

Samara had not prayed since her childhood but she made a silent prayer now: "Let it be Anthony."

The guard sullenly motioned the two women to another doorway. A barred window allowed the late sunlight to pour in.

The room they were ushered to was sunlit as well and the sight of it cheered Samara slightly. As for Dilys, she sank down into the only chair in the room and lay her head on a table, just missing an inkstand and set of quills.

Samara could not sit down even if there had been a chair. This window was tighter and stronger than the other, the bars unquestionably stronger. But there was something heavenly about the golden sky and Samara clung to the hope that it was an omen.

Dilys disturbed her thoughts. "That fellow in the doorway keeps watching me."

276

"He is appointed to watch you," Samara said impatiently. "He is a guard."

Then she heard footsteps and for a minute her heart almost stopped beating. Was it possible she could recognise Anthony's footsteps?

Then he came into the room accompanied by another guard whose hand was tight around his arm. His hands were still tied behind him but – thanks be to God! – he looked very much himself.

She heard herself cry hoarsely, "My God! My God!"

He grinned. "No. Only myself. Are you all right, darling? How have they treated you?"

With an eye on the guard she forced a smile too. "They were very kind. I was worried about you."

"May I embrace the lady, just once?" Anthony asked the guard.

The guard shook his head but looked as though he wished he might say yes.

Anthony shrugged. "Well, later, perhaps."

Samara reached out to touch him, then, fearing the anger of the guard, merely caressed Anthony's sleeve. His eyes, with their bright humour, told her he understood. He looked as if he had been in a battle of some kind, his clothing in disarray, bloodstains from scratches over his torn shirt. His jacket was gone, but the officer explained in English, "The signor made trouble for our men while the gypsy boy escaped."

Dilys cried out in delight, "Then he will rescue me . . . us."

Samara groaned, guessing this would add to Anthony's crimes. Her only consolation came from

277

the officer standing in the doorway. He told Samara in a more conciliating tone, "If the signor speaks the truth, the young gypsy will bring help to assist the signor. The Vatican is dealing with the signor's banking house in London with connections in Rome. The signor here says he is acquainted with our friend, Signor Cunningham. A matter of rebuilding certain monuments across the Tiber. If – I only say if – the Signor speaks for you, all may yet be well. Signor Linden's papers are then verified."

Samara closed her eyes briefly in her relief. She reached for the chair Dilys had left in her excitement and leaned against it to regain her equilibrium.

Anthony called angrily, "Help her, someone!"

She smiled tiredly, waved away the officer. "Nonsense! We aren't out of our troubles yet. Suppose Alexi runs away instead of bringing Mr Cunningham?"

There was an awkward silence. Then Dilys swung around, outraged. "How dare you say that? Alexi would die for me. He's said so a thousand times."

Samara exchanged looks with Anthony who, she suspected, was putting the best face on things. No one even knew if Mr Cunningham had reached Rome yet.

Anthony said, "Oh, Alexi's not a bad fellow. Besides, the Cunningham apartments are near the Spanish Steps, not too far from where—" He hesitated, "—where Alexi escaped from the tumbril. With the reward promised to him, he was anxious to get out and be on as fast as possible to the Spanish Steps."

The officer did not smile, but he seemed both amused and rueful.

"The Signor Linden caused a disturbance as they came to the gates here and by the time we had gotten him, the gypsy was gone."

Samara muttered "Good God!"

The officer seemed to regard her words as natural, in the circumstances.

"If the Signor Cunningham does not arrive, I very much fear Sir Anthony – if that is his name – will have another charge against him."

Alexi. A slender reed to depend upon, Samara thought. And meanwhile, here was Anthony with his hands doubtless numb behind him, waiting for Alexi, of all people, to save him.

Samara moved the chair out and motioned Anthony to be seated. He hesitated, glanced at the officer who nodded, and then he more or less fell into the edge of the chair and sighed with relief.

Samara said uneasily. "What if Alexi doesn't come back? How long are we to wait before we know what is to be done with us?"

Anthony was trying to chafe his hands behind him but he looked at the officer. To Samara's susprise the officer was suddenly smiling.

"They are back. And with Signor Cunningham. Evidently, that gentleman is in Rome at this moment. I have excellent hearing. And then, too, our Papal officers saw to it that the boy reached his destination."

"You had Alexi followed?" asked Anthony, a little angry. "If I had known, I wouldn't have worried so much."

"You hear that?" the officer asked.

279

It was obvious now. There were voices in the outer passage and Samara leaned against the wall, feeling ice-cold in the middle of the Roman spring heat. Mr Cunningham himself hurried into the room crying, "My dear fellow! My very dear fellow! This can't be. We were dining when your gypsy boy burst in. Where is he? Here, you!" To the guard. "Fetch in the gypsy. And those with him. You don't know my dinner guest, Sir Anthony, but we were discussing business in which the London bank with whom you deal is involved."

"Do not mind that," Samara burst out. "Untie him."

The officer who had been comforting the prisoners murmured, "Not quite yet, Sir Anthony. First, there must be the testimony of the gentlemen from the banking house."

Samara was more intent upon untying Anthony than in listening to technicalities, but her fingers felt too clumsy and the silent guard who had been so surly now came forward and tried to shove her away, saying something in Italian. She was struggling with him, which seemed to strike Anthony as humorous, but Cunningham, unmindful of his client's discomfort, went on: "I've brought my dinner guest with me. Saved him from that intolerable Lenten diet he insists upon." He raised his voice. "You there, Alexi! That is your name? Please escort my friend to Sir Anthony."

With growing astonishment, Samara watched as an ascetic-looking man, dressed elegantly in pure black and white, entered with a proud Alexi. Mr Cunningham introduced the gentleman as the Signor d'Abruzzi. "He has the ear of the Vatican in our bank's dealings over repairs across the Tiber."

Signor d'Abruzzi bowed, offered his hand to Anthony, then, seeing the prisoner's bound and reddened hands, begged his pardon stiffly. He spoke in excellent English.

"My good friend, Signor Cunningham, will show you correspondence between your British banking concern and the Vatican, mentioning that you might be visiting Rome and identifying you, Sir Anthony, by a miniature painted with considerable exactness by one of your associates in London, so that there could be no mistake when you arrived. As you know, we are plagued with considerable criminal activity in Southern Italy upon the high roads. Do you remember the matter, Excellency?"

"I suppose I do," Anthony admitted, "but I was in a great hurry when I left England and I am very sorry to say, I didn't wait for the letter and miniature."

The officer of the Papal States nodded to the guard and this time the matter of Anthony's bound hands was attended to. Then the officer leaned over the miniature and accompanying letter. He said in his wry way, "It is a pity we were not given the portrait when the matter of your arrest occurred on board ship. Naturally, if you are vouched for by the Vatican . . ."

Samara felt as though she wanted to faint with relief, but she recovered her wits, partly inspired by Dilys who clapped her hands.

"I knew he must be innocent. And think! If it had

not been for Alexi, Cousin Anthony might have remained in a dungeon forever."

Anthony sighed. "Gentlemen, I have a great favour to ask. May I go to some decent place and take a bath?"

The Papal officer looked at Signor d'Abruzzi.

"I fear Sir Anthony will not be able to leave Rome just yet, but it is only a technicality. There is the matter of the gypsy Dominguez's death and the theft of those valuable coins. Obviously, no one would accuse Sir Anthony. Not with the Vatican to witness his character, but . . ."

"What?" Cunningham asked in surprise. "That theft on board ship concerned Miss Samara's coins? But weren't they stolen from the two of you by that gypsy who vanished with them?"

"A fellow named Dominguez," Anthony put in. "He mentioned them to the captain and some officers on the ship. Probably in his cups. But it would seem the officers are responsible for their loss."

The Papal officer said regretfully, "We were told this by Sir Anthony, but unfortunately, we had no way of knowing he spoke the truth. I regret to say, they may never be recovered. I was told something like an hour ago that the ship has taken off without clearance. Whether we may be able to persuade the government of the Two Sicilies to return them, we cannot say."

"Then," Signor d'Abruzzi reminded him with quiet severity, "may we trust that with the Vatican to vouch for Sir Anthony, he will shortly be out of his difficulties?"

Samara and Anthony looked at each other, not daring to smile. They knew what the answer would be and were too grateful to remind anyone of their false imprisonment.

The officer gave the guard a quick command in Italian and bowed to Signor d'Abruzzi.

"We are always anxious to avoid a miscarriage of justice, Excellency, thanks to Your Excellency's efforts."

As d'Abruzzi and the Papal representative discussed Anthony's narrow escape, Samara tried to bring life to Anthony's numb fingers while he objected, complaining that he couldn't kiss her, or even put his arms around her, and would she please hurry to rectify things?

Alexi who was locked in Dilys's arms, reminded Anthony over the girl's tousled head, "Sir Anthony, am I still to receive the money you promised me for fetching Signor Cunningham?"

Dilys was airy about it. "Oh, Cousin will pay, won't you, Cousin? He is very honest."

Anthony said, "Certainly. I will take it out of the worth of my missing ruby set."

That left Dilys speechless for a minute. Having recovered the use of his fingers, Anthony took Samara into his arms.

"Darling, I'm awfully afraid you may have seen the last of your coins."

How comfortable it was to be in his arms!

"What coins?" she asked.